SPLIT THE SUN

AN INHERIT THE STARS NOVEL

Tessa Elwood

RP|TEENS
PHILADELPHIA

ISBN 978-0-7624-5847-9
Library of Congress Control Number: 2016940454
E-book ISBN 978-0-7624-6124-0

10 9 8 7 6 5 4 3 2 1
Digit on the right indicates the number of this printing

Designed by Frances J. Soo Ping Chow
Edited by Andrea Cascardi
Typography: AgencyFB, Lato, Matchmaker, and Mercury

Running Press Book Publishers
2300 Chestnut Street
Philadelphia, PA 19103–4371

Visit us on the web!
www.runningpress.com/rpkids

For biscuits and gravy, bats,
and mushrooms. Daffodils,
Elvis, and stockings. Or rather,
loyalty, strength, and love.

MY SANDAL IS INTENT ON DESTRUCTION. IT slides off my foot and drops eighteen stories. Maybe it longs to be lethal, kill a pedestrian. Add another death to the family tally. Nine instead of ten.

Rack 'em up.

The museum roof is ringed in a high stone wall for leaning against. Or standing upon. It's warm underfoot, wide and sturdy. Too sturdy. Too safe.

I lean into the dark.

Below, the city pulses. It has a heartbeat. Groaning hoverbuses, sporadic horns, skytower ad-screens blitzing neon. The Galton House capital in all its glory. A planet of city, continents of steel. It's long after midnight, or one, or even two, but the air still sweats—beads my neck and shoulders— thick as the haze that swallows the sky.

Yonni, my gran, used to talk about stars. How she'd lie in the grass on some backwater planet, and count the glow-dotted infinity. She'd lose her place after a solid thousand or two.

Ain't nothin' like 'em, Kit. You can see God up there.

Here, there's only smog.

No, excuse me, a soft, hazy shimmer. This *is* Low South, heart of the historic district. Lordlings kill to live in the surrounding cloudsuites towers—where air is mountain fresh and pure as spring.

Not that any of them know what mountains look like, or spring, unless they channel their money into off-planet travel—or grew up somewhere else. Yonni had seen mountains. She had a hidden fund for the day when she would show me, too. She promised.

Like she swore she was feeling better a whole hour before she died.

A breeze curls past my ankles to kiss the distant street. Catches a napkin or cup and tumbles it end over end. The walkway is empty of people and bodies. My sandal didn't kill anyone. The tally stands at nine.

Mom would be so disappointed.

I kick off my other shoe. The ledge is cracked, the stone rough, and I slide my toes over its cragged lip. Close my eyes. There is nothing beyond the pads of my feet, the press of the air. Distant traffic fading out.

You understand why I can't keep you on, Mr. Remmings said hours ago, after eviscerating me in front of the entire staff. I thought that'd be the end of it, but no, he had to follow me to my locker. Spell it out. *The museum cannot be*

6

associated with hack-bombers or threats, and your mother—

Kills people. Killed people.

Humidity coats my skin. My arms hang and I let them float apart, lift a little. Except I don't have wings and I don't want to fly.

Mom would always pull my hands together when I was small, cup my palms between her big ones. *You've the whole world right here*, she'd say, *what will you do with it?*

I dunno, give it back?

My hands were empty then. They still are.

Nine is useless as a tally. I hated being nine. By nine, Mom had been gone a year and Dad a month before the landlord figured out I was alone.

Ten is better.

On my tenth birthday, Yonni found me.

I lower my arms. The world shrinks to the crags in my chest and the stone underfoot. Everything is quiet— my heart, the city. The world open, beckoning. Silence. So much space.

I step forward.

A steel arm grabs my waist and yanks me back onto the rooftop. I ram my elbow into a hard chest, someone grunts and the hold breaks.

I sprint five steps and spin, fists raised and blood pumping backward.

A man stands where I was, pale and old—forty maybe—with thick arms and stubby fingers that catch the light.

"What the hell was that?" he yells. "You trying to get yourself killed?"

My lungs race with my gasping heart, and I don't say a word.

He shouldn't be here; no one should be here. The rooftop door is locked, and maybe I know how to pop it, but no one else ever has.

Except the man doesn't wear the green museum uniform, but the near-black stripes of a power technician. The city has been rife with power-outs lately, and we've even had to cancel tours. Mr. Remmings probably called him in.

The man steps forward, head high and finger pointing. "This area is off-limits, you can't—" He pauses, close now, and squints. "Wait, I know you."

My breath stops.

Of course. Even here, somebody knows me. And it's not even *me*, it's the straight black hair and bony arms, the sharp nose and chin. Chiseled: the girl version.

You used to look more like Ricky, you know, Mom said once, when she took me out for coffee to try mothering on for size. *Now we could be sisters.*

The man is in my face, taller, but not by much. "You were on the feeds. You're the daughter."

Not *whose* daughter. Mom bombed the House Archive tower and destroyed half a city block. Quantifiers aren't needed.

I don't answer. I don't look away, either.

His mouth flatlines under grim eyes. He moves back to the ledge and looks down, as if a flightwing waited to catch me. "You meeting her or something? She here?"

"She's dead," I say, and he snorts.

Because of course the brilliant Millie Oen—Archivist, data-technologist, and now murderous bomber—couldn't possibly have died in the explosion she caused. She was too smart for that. The rescue teams couldn't find her body.

Though with the extent of the explosion, they couldn't find her lab, her office, or any of the sublevel libraries and record-storage floors, either. They melted into each other. The Archive was our digital core, the central data structure all networks fed into and out of. Reports, power-grids, birth records, histories, and finances from mundane to high clearance, the Archive held it all—and Mom erased it in a night.

Our House is running on backups.

"So what was this?" The power technician asks, waving at the ledge, the street. "Atonement?"

"I didn't set the bomb," I say.

"You didn't stop it," he says, and there's no fighting that. *I didn't know* doesn't change anything.

I should have known. I was in her lab that night. I should have *known*.

I move to the stairwell.

"Where the hell are you going?" the man calls.

"Somewhere less populated," I say and slam the door.

EVERYWHERE'S POPULATED. THE PREDAWN CLEAN-
ing crews own the streets, their man-size sweeper bugs
flashing lights and whirring low. I could step out in front
of one, but all I'd get is scrubbed raw. The woman walking
with the nearest sweeper glares. She's either read my mind
or I'm in the way.

Or else she's registered my face and added two and two
together, like the power technician.

Freakin' newsfeeds. They ran a report on Mom, her history, and her surviving relatives. The obligatory *this is how
you grow a crazed murderer* special. The lack of real information was a testament in itself—either to bad reporting or
Mom's skill in masking truth—but there's one thing they did
get right.

Me.

A whole five-minute segment with my face front and
center. Not that they had much on me, either. Kreslyn
Franks, eighteen, youngest tour guide on record for the
Gilken Museum Foundation. I'm wearing the uniform in the
picture, which they must have pulled from the museum's
feedpage on the general network. No mention of Yonni or
Dad, or a life outside work. Yonni was a master at keeping
her private life private—a prerequisite for anyone working
nights in other people's beds. And Dad? The newscasters'
guess is as good as mine.

As far as the life part, well, that's none of their business.

The glaring street cleaner waves over another of the crew, then leans in and whispers in his ear. His gaze locks with mine. Surprise, anger, a touch terrified at the edges.

Lovely.

I duck into an alley and sprint to the next street over. More cleaners and traffic. At this rate, the only point of isolation would be home. So I walk. Barefoot.

The skytowers block most of their namesake, but some light leaks through—changing from pitch to pale, skipping soft. The pavement simmers and dirt coats my soles in the patches the sweepers missed. Low South blends into South Central, age-old towers butting against color and height, and then morphs into the respectable West 6th district, and finally into the haggard-but-standing West 1st.

West 1st used to be deeply monied and highly sought after, until fifty-story cloudsuites became the thing. None of our suitetowers have over fifteen. Mine has ten. A squat, little stone-and-steel number with more windows than wall space. Wide paved steps, still austere despite their cracks, lead up to an ornate glass door. I'm halfway across the street before the deeper shadows by the entryway register as human form.

Dee, Dad's sister.

She's in her favorite black jacket with the pink studs,

dangling a cigarette and blowing smoke rings. Perfect circles that expand the higher they get, to entrap the sky.

If there was any justice, they'd slip around her throat and squeeze.

"Where you been?" she calls.

I climb the steps and pull my keypass out of my pocket, keeping as far from her as possible. "What's it to you?"

"Don't be like that." She all but drips sugar, even as her next smoke ring hits my ear. "Thought you'd be happy to see me."

Yeah, six months ago, when it might have made a difference for Yonni. When it might have made a difference for everything.

I slap my keypass to the hidden security reader in the wall, melded in to look like stone. Its tiny light flashes green, and I push through the heavy glass door. The ancient lobby arcs with wide brown carpet before narrowing to a resident hall, and ending at the rickety elevator. No furniture anymore, not even a desk.

Dee slips in before I can stop her, flicking her cigarette away as the door closes.

If she thinks I'm letting her into Yonni's suite, she has another think coming. I plant my feet and cross my arms.

"God, you look like Ricky when you do that," says Dee.

Which probably beats looking like Mom, but not by

much. At least Dad never killed anyone. That I know of.

"What do you want, Dee?"

"To have a civil conversation, is that so hard?"

My nails bite skin. If she wanted civil, she shouldn't have slammed the door in my face the first and last time I asked her for help. Real help. Yonni was sick, Central Medical wouldn't approve her treatment without more money than we had, and Yonni was out of pills. Greg, my cousin, could have fixed that problem. He has contacts. Lord knows, he deals in every other pill on the planet. At least these were legal. Except when I opened the door to his place, I got Dee.

Her jaw tightens, fist curling, and I shift for the blow. Dee has a mean one. But she doesn't swing, she smiles. "You know Greg's trying to ditch that life. I couldn't let you slam him right back into it."

Yeah, at the time he was trying so hard that I'd found him splashing naked in Low South's water channel. I'd dug up his clothes and hauled him off the main thoroughfare before the City Enactors showed up, while he waffled between laughing, trying to eat my hair, and searching my pockets for more pills. Not that Dee knows that. Greg and I never told each other's secrets, back when we were close enough to have secrets to share.

"Besides, I don't know why you're still harping on that," Dee says, "it's not like you didn't get the pills without Greg."

Our eyes lock. Dee's a mask with a smile, and I can't tell if she is fishing or knows how I pulled it off.

If she knew, she'd have made use of it.

All for pills that didn't even work.

If the power technician had just minded his own business, I wouldn't be stuck in this conversation right now.

"What do you want, Dee?" I ask again.

She pulls another cigarette from her pocket and lights up. "Greg needs Mom's place."

Yonni's place. Mine.

"No," I say.

She dangles her burning cig, ash floating to the carpet. "The suite is mine by right, and I'm giving it to him. I know Mom's death hit you hard, so I've given you grace. But it's been six months and that stops now. I want Greg in by the end of the week. You can take it up with him if you stick around or not." She shrugs, even grins. "You two used to get on well. I'm sure if you pay rent, he'll work something out."

So sure, so matter-of-fact, as if she has a leg to stand on. And she might, but for one key point.

"Yonni left me the suite," I say.

She leans in, eyes very wide, soft brown rimmed in purple. She's soft all over, rounded chin and puffy cheeks. Angelic even, on a good day. "I'm the oldest, and by Right of Inheritance all Mom's things are mine."

"That only works when there's no will," I say. "Yonni's is at the Records Office. Look it up."

"She was too sick to know what she was signing."

But Dee already tried that line when the will was read and got nowhere.

I open the lobby door and throw out a smile as soft as hers. "Good seeing you."

Her lips thin, but only a little, her voice husky soft. "I didn't want to tell you this, what with your mother's recent little incident—"

"You mean, blowing up a national icon and its night crew?"

"But Greg *needs* this suite. He has to have a steady job and permanent address, and he's running out of time. The City Enactors are after him."

"Aren't they always?"

Her hands twitch like she could spear her nails through my neck. She doesn't, though. Point to Dee.

"Just give them yours," I say. "Isn't he staying with you?"

"My place is only zoned for one occupant. My landlord would kick me out."

"Since when did you move to a singles suitetower?"

"What do you care?" she shoots back. "Greg will lose everything without a home base. He needs Mom's suite."

Greg is forever on the verge of losing everything. Even if he wasn't, Yonni laid down the law so close to her death it was practically a last rite. *Don't you dare let Dee and her worthless spawn in my place—not even a foot inside, you hear me? Give me your word.*

And I had.

"He'll land on his feet." I pull the door wider. "He always does."

Her hands clench, but she fights it. "You don't understand."

"The suite's mine, it's on record. Go home."

She straightens in slow motion. "Fine then, ruin his life— but don't expect any favors from me." She flicks her cig at my bare feet. Her aim's perfect, but I'm faster—jumping back and releasing the door. She grabs it before it swings shut, shoots me a perfect Franks smile over her shoulder, then slips through and slams it behind her. The echo booms; the door frame shakes.

I wait in the resulting quiet. The whole first floor must have heard that, probably the next three up. Old Mrs. Divs at the very least. I glance down the hall to the first suite door on the left. No gray head pops out, wanting to know what all the fuss is over. Maybe she slept through it.

Maybe she doesn't get out of bed for anything less than the House Lord's death. We were all up for that one. Even ancient Mr. Sana, wandering the hall in only his socks and boxers, repeating nothing but "Lord Galton, Lord

Galton" over and over. A couple of years ago, it was "Lady Galton, Lady Galton," when the now late Lord's mother died. Rumor had it her son poisoned her so he could gain his inheritance and control our House.

He certainly could have. Lord Galton was a ruthless bastard of the first order, but not subtle enough for poison. When Yonni started a betting pool on who killed the Lady—members of the ruling House family never die unaided—I put my money on Lord Galton's wife, Lady Genevieve. Blonde, gorgeous, and forever smiling on the feeds with the perfect gracious response? Absolutely.

Yonni laughed and the rest of the residents rolled their eyes, but Mrs. Divs backed me up. Put two reds on Lady G. *I like a long shot*, she'd said.

Two weeks ago, when Lord Galton died, no one took bets on anything. The Lord had no children, so our House has no Heir. No ruler. Lady Genevieve married into the family, but she isn't "of" the family—wasn't born into it. Only bloodlings can rule. The late Lord had no siblings, neither did his mother. Or her mother, come to that. The Enactors are searching for the surviving bloodling Heir, but if the family line has died . . . I don't know what will happen. At least Yonni won't have to see it.

She didn't have to see Mom's stunt, either. Guess there's an upside to everything.

No one comes to chew me out for Dee's racket, so I ditch the lobby for the stairwell. I swear something died in the elevators once, and you can always spot visitors by who hits the call button.

The fifth-floor hallway matches levels one through ten—a universal drab brown except for the digiswitchprint walls with their stock designs. Stripes, dots, or florals that used to change every week. They've been dark since the first power-out after the Archive blew.

My suite's the fourth door on the left. I swap the building's keypass for my personal one and let myself in.

Yonni's place opens on a mini hall that turns into a big living room. The suite is mostly living room, with a small open kitchen off to the right and a narrow bedroom door to the left. Minimal furniture, a couple of bare bookshelves that used to hold mementos. Tiny, pretty things that held surprising value because Missa, Yonni's last lover, never gave shoddy gifts. They all reflected Yonni in a dozen little ways.

I would know. I pawned them all.

I round the island countertop and enter the kitchen. It's small but smoothly compact.

My flipcom buzzes in my pocket.

Dee probably, needing a second last word.

I open the icer, slide out my flipcom, and press it to my ear as I reach for the juice. "What?"

"Miss Franks?" asks a clipped, professional, male voice.

Great.

I press my forehead against the icer's chill inner shelf. It burns. "Yeah?"

"Is this Kreslyn Franks?"

"What do you need?" I ask.

"This is the Investigative Enactment Office. We have a few questions for you. Could you come into our main branch tomorrow at eight?"

I close my eyes.

This was coming. I knew this was coming. It's been three days since the Archive, and no one's come banging on the door.

I'm Millie Oen's daughter and the last person to see her alive. Probably.

Not that they know that.

I don't think.

My palms burn, but my mouth's dry. "Okay. Yeah, I'll be there."

"Thank you, we appreciate your cooperation." His pitch is perfect, a recording-level quality.

He hangs up.

The juice jug chills my palm, weighs as much as a tower. The flipcom in my other hand could double for a brick. I set both in the icer and close the door, which brings me face-to-face with my magnetized quotepad. A two-year anniversary gift for being the Gilken Museum's most *dedicated and reliable tour guide*. I was on the fast track for a scholarship. *The* scholarship that would get me off-planet. Scholar Gilken set it up himself, two hundred and eight years ago, for anyone who wanted to learn. And the scholarship still has funds because Gilken built the data system our House still runs on—he founded and oversaw the creation of the official House Archive.

The one Mom blew up.

The quotepad blazes its cheery yellow. *"All data, mundane and divine, is a grand investigative saga. Not to uncover why a man has died; but the darker secret of why he lives."*

"Easy." I hit the power and the screen goes dark. "He never had the guts to jump."

THE CITY HATES MORNINGS, SO I END UP AT THE MAR-ket—probably the only open place in Low South. It buzzes with off-school kids, lunching professionals, and the ancient in their hoverchairs. The unending line of shop windows sport digital models that flex and smile, morphing from one outfit to the next. Overhead, stringed bulb lights bounce and shimmer under the massive cooling fans. Each fan doubles me in height, blades wide and near silent. Perhaps even sharp. Though at that height and speed, they wouldn't have to be.

Huh.

I refocus on the street and almost run into the Brink kids. They're out in full force today, huddled in a yellow mass near the Market's arched entrance. Their digitized shirts blink protests across their chests, while a projector spins words against passing shoppers. *Stop wasting energy*, and *You won't gut us to fuel your markets*.

The kids match the digital words with spoken ones. Energy is running out. We killed all independent planets outside House borders by extracting fuel from their cores. And once we burn through that garnered energy, where do we think the next batch will come from? Right now, planets on the Brink are rationed down to five hours of energy a day, while here we gawk at nonstop ad-screens and control the temperature *outside*.

And there's the flaw. If our House was really amid an "energy crisis," somebody would turn the cooling fans off. This may be an upscale market, but it's not like lordlings shop here.

One of them spots me, a tall guy in a skin-tight black shirt and heavy eyebrows that flatline over his nose as he stares. And stares. He has that look, like the woman in the corner grocery yesterday, or the power technician this morning on the roof.

I know you. You're her.

I duck into the nearest side street, then circle through an open-air restaurant toward the public elevators at the far end. The best part of Low South isn't the hours or the shops; it's the walkways. High glass paths with thin rails that criss-cross from one skytower to the next.

Best of all, they hang above the cooling fans.

Up here the blades move too fast to track, creating an empty sheen that carries power. More, a promise. *You won't feel this.*

I grab the silver railing. It's thin and high, with no room to sit, stand, or waver. I'll have to vault it, jump out just far enough. A beat and done. It'd be over.

Except for the breakfasting crowd below, who'd end up with blood all over their eggs.

And nightmares for life.

Wouldn't that be a legacy? Maybe not quite the terror of Mom's, but close enough.

My hands slide off the rail and I slide to the floor, cross my legs above the smudged glass. Below the fan spins, close, almost touchable. Taunting.

"Shut up," I say. It doesn't.

Farther down, at ground level, everyone gets on with their lives. Everyone unconcerned, or else desperate and hiding it well. Enjoying the cooling fans while ignoring the blades. No one looks up, except a dark-haired guy by the fountain who stares or seems to. A thick mop covers his ears and his eyes, but his neck cranes back as if he's blissed out or asleep or both. Either way, he'll wake up starved.

Come to that, so am I.

Market breakfasts try to rival cloudsuite prices, but Mr. Remmings did count out the money he owed me to the last red before kicking me out. A methodical chant in front of the whole staff, so no one could say the museum didn't do right by their employees.

Even me.

"YOU'RE KRESLYN FRANKS."

I look up from my plate of eggy noodled joy. Mr. Skin-tight Shirt with Abs has tracked me down and brought company. They flank my perfect cube of a table on all sides except mine.

I don't think there's anyone behind me. I don't turn to look.

"Correct me if I'm wrong," says T-shirt guy, sliding into the chair opposite, "But I'm not wrong."

A blonde girl with the double topknots slips in the chair to my right, while a skinny guy takes the left seat. Skinny's yellow shirt flashes SAVE THE BRINK in neon red. It's not a good look on him. The girl has more muscles than both boys together, which is an excellent look on her. The trio lean back in casual coordination, sharing looks and tapping fingers.

I lay down my fork.

Skin-tight Abs leans in, both elbows on the table. "Your mother is a god."

My mouth opens and I—have no idea where to go from here. "My . . . *mother* blew up the Archive."

He grins. "Yes. She did."

Waking up this morning was a bad idea. Or was it yesterday morning? One of those.

Ordering breakfast was definitely stupid.

I lean back in my seat. "What do you want?"

"Millie Oen."

Him and everyone else.

"She's dead," I say.

His smile gains an edge. "You sure?"

Here we go.

"What do you want?" I repeat, slower this time.

"She cleansed us," says the skinny one. He's got a pretty mouth and an open face and eyes that are almost reverent. They spark.

My heart jabs the terror button. "Cleansed."

"The bloodlings," says Skinny, "we don't know who they are anymore. They don't exist."

"No, they just haven't been found," I say.

Abs presses close enough that he could eat my noodles for me. "Don't worry, we're on your side."

Oh, good. I have a side.

"Can you reach your mother?" the girl whispers, her elbows on the table, too. "Without them noticing?"

Them?

"We need her," says Abs.

"She can save us," the skinny one chimes in. The kid can't be that old. His voice sounds like he's six, but his eyes look fifty.

"The *Brink* needs her," Skin-tight adds.

The girl's elbow brushes mine, her breath licking my hair. "Can you get her a message?"

"Absolutely," I say. "Find me a spirit talker, I'll slit my wrist, and we can open a death channel."

The girl growls, and I can almost feel her teeth grind. "This isn't a game."

"What, really?" I face her head-on, and our noses brush. Perfect kissing distance. She flinches, unprepared. Apparently, *she* is the only one who gets to breathe down people's necks. I lean that much closer. "Mom's a murderer and you're calling her a god, so tell me—what exactly is this, then?"

She shifts, straightens. Something flashes silver in my peripheral, though her eyes never leave mine. Something that hums like a spark blade.

That was fast. Impressive. She could give Greg a run for his money.

She's assuming I have something left to lose.

A massive clatter rocks the pavilion. Everyone jumps, turns—the girl, too, twisting around. I lean sideways for a better view.

Three tables over, an overturned chair barricades an upended tray, which rattles against the courtyard's inter-locked stone tile. A guy, the mop-headed guy who was watching the fans, stands amid the mess, swearing. A couple seated nearby pull their shoes away from the pool of his drink, while he apologizes profusely and grabs napkins—knocking over another chair in the process. Boy is definitely blissed out. He tosses his bangs and glances up across the dining pavilion, straight at me.

Our eyes lock.

Strike that, the boy is stone sober and knows exactly what he's about. He glances behind me, then back. Two seconds. Then he's yelling for more napkins and trying to pat down the closest couple's shoes.

Everyone at my table is riveted, the girl's eyes narrowing as her knife hand dangles at her side under the table. Forgotten.

Gutted in the Market by crazy people probably isn't a prime way to go.

I slide from my chair and bolt.

I SWING INTO AN ALLEY OFF A SIDE STREET, PRESS into the wall, and peer around the corner like I'm in some feed-network show. The thoroughfare races with street-hovers, low-level flightwing traffic, and a suited group of striding people with their flipcoms out.

No guys flashing abs or girls in topknots. No mop-heads, either.

I sink into the alley wall. The stone burns.

Everyone is crazy.

"You set that up?" I ask the tower-cluttered sky. "Seeing as you're a god and all, want to tell me which contingent was yours?"

Mom doesn't answer, but my money's on the Brinkers. Mom would probably get a kick out of being considered divine. She had the looks for it—dark hair, dark eyes, and power. Sharp chin, sharp shoulders, sharp suit. She'd sat at her desk when I walked in, her Archive office twice the size of Yonni's suite. She didn't stand or fidget or cross her arms. Didn't even register surprise, as if I was still the bawling nine-year-old she'd abandoned eight years before.

I see you found me, she said.

Yeah. I'd marched right up and flattened both palms on her desk. *And you're going to wish I hadn't*.

She'd smiled. A beautiful, lovely thing. Very knowing, as if I'd be the one to regret.

29

A godlike smile to match the skinny kid's eyes.

I rub my shoulders, sweat-soaked and sticky, and turn deeper into the alley. Head north toward home.

A MAN SITS ON THE STEPS OF MY SUITETOWER. HEAD bowed, elbows on knees, flask hanging between loose fingers. Sandy hair to match his sandy skin. Broad shoulders framed by the wide steps' rusting rail.

If he doesn't look up, maybe I won't know him.

If I'm not here, he'll go away.

I step back. He looks up, head lulling, eyes red and puffy.

My father grins. "There's my girl."

"Dad," I say.

He beckons me closer. I don't move.

He's thinner than he was three years ago. Smaller. Or maybe I'm the one who has grown. His bones protrude from the wrists beneath his sleeves, knuckles bright under tight skin.

Last I'd heard, he was two planets over, with Melodie or Amalie or some other -ie with hair as dark as Mom's. But that was long before Yonni died.

I tried to find him when Yonni got sick, when the money ran out and her meds were almost gone. I tracked him to a place he'd been six months ago, even got a flipcom number some past lover swore still worked. It didn't.

Either that or he didn't answer.

Dad holds out his arms.

I cross mine. "What do you want?"

31

"To see my baby." He smiles. Sweet, open, and a little busted.

There are advantages to being Millie Oen's daughter. My smile beats his to hell. "I'm sorry, visiting hours are over."

I climb the steps, bypassing his.

He snags my hand, squeezing tight, arm stretching, until I have to stop. "Don't be like that."

I don't squeeze back. Worse, I don't pull away. His hands are as big as they ever were. He could lift and swing both Greg and me at once when we were little. From the intensity of his current hold, maybe he still could.

"I heard about Mom," he says. His mom, not mine. Yonni.

When? I ask, almost scream in my head. *When she died? When I sent message after message? When I would have begged on my knees for you to show?*

I grab the railing for leverage, palm to rust to steel, and don't say a word.

The "when" doesn't matter. Not anymore.

"Must have been hard on you," he says, "losing her like that. I'm sorry I—"

I yank free of him, push up the last two steps to the door.

Dad clambers to unsteady feet and reaches for me again. "Baby doll—"

I press back against the door, just out of grasp. "I'm not one of your girls, Dad."

"You are my baby, though." He goes for the patented Franks puppy-eyed look, as if I'm unaware of the con. His reaching hand finds my elbow. "I can't imagine what it's been like for you, especially lately—I mean, your *mother*. Who'd have thought?—but you can trust me, right? I love you, baby. I'm here for you."

Right. Just like he was when I was nine, when I was alone in a house with no power and nowhere to go. I squeeze past him and slam my keypass against the security reader. Push through the door and slam it shut as his blotchy palms hit the glass.

"Kit!" Muffled through the glass. "Don't do this."

"Watch me." I back up, turn for the elevator.

"I'm sorry!" he wails. The words break and my step falters. I falter—heart heavy, breath shallow.

"I know I should have come back when Mom—when she—God, I know, Kit. I *know*. If I could take it back I would. You're all I have, baby. You know that, right? You're all I've got."

Skin squeaks against glass, slides down. A hand? Fingertips? I half raise my palms to cover my ears, but that never worked years ago when Mom and Dad fought. Besides, I'm not a baby anymore.

Or a damn baby doll.

I glance over my shoulder.

33

Dad's on the ground, and the glass is streaked from his hand or the snot from his nose. He's shiny red as a marzinberri. Heaving quiet, sincere sobs that twist my gut. "We're family, Kit," he says, or I think he says. The glass muffles everything. "We're family. I've nowhere else to go."

We were family six months ago, when he wouldn't call me back.

Dad crumples, like so much chopped meat.

I can't let him in. Yonni would kill me. I'd lose the suite. She wrote it into her will, blocked Dad out right along with Dee and Greg. If I let any of my family stay overnight, the place is forfeited, the will rescinded. The Record Officials could march in and kick me out.

Dad's crying. The sun catches every awkward tear.

The Records Office never makes random tower-calls. They'll never know.

Yonni will know.

I can't fail her any more than I have already. She's dead.

We're family, Kit.

I kick the carpet, spin back around, and open the door. Dad falls onto the lobby floor.

"One night," I say. "Tomorrow, you're gone."

His eyes light up. He stands, pulls me in a hug of alcohol and sweat. "Oh, baby, I love you. I love you, baby doll."

"Whatever," I say. "Let's get you upstairs."

MOM AND I BRACKET YONNI'S BED—HER ON ONE SIDE, ME on the other. Not a proper bed, but a raised tube braced with smaller tubes for fluid drainage. It takes up most of the tiny room, leaving us to squeeze into what's left. The air hangs stuffy, metallic. A little sweet, a little burnt.

Mom props her feet on one of the lower tubes, ankles crossed under loose slacks, shiny shoes tapered to black points. Twin soles against the pale isolation of Yonni.

I stare at Mom's unmoving feet and then into her perfect heart face—rounded cheeks, sharp chin—the memory crisp despite the dream. Or because of it.

And I am dreaming.

"Wake up," I tell her or me or both. "Just wake up."

Nothing happens. The room doesn't blink out, I don't open my eyes somewhere else.

But I can always wake myself up.

"Have you ever seen the future, Kit?" Mom's head tilts with her toes, which swing this way and that. "And I don't mean the Accounting. Have you ever had a moment, where without any evidence whatsoever, you just knew?"

I lean across Yonni's encased silence, careful not to smudge the glass bed. "Get your damn shoes off her bed."

"What if I said you were my moment?"

I stand, slamming the chair back into the wall as I point to the door. "Out."

35

She doesn't rise or even jump, simply fishes in her pocket and pulls out a small datadisc. Holds it out over Yonni's chest, dangled between loose red nails.

I grab her wrist. "What are you doing?"

"Rewriting the grid," she says and lets the disc fall.

I open my eyes. Above, the white ceiling cracks from corner to corner, connecting the stained tiles. Soft light filters through the window.

Yonni's bedroom. Mine now.

I sit up, rub my head to smear the words. It didn't happen that way. Nothing happened that way.

Except the glass bed, which became a casket when the treatment failed. I can still feel it, the sterile room's stuffy air, the sweet metallic under my tongue.

Snores filter through the door to the living room. Dad passed out maybe five minutes after I dumped him on the couch. Didn't move all day or all night, it sounds like.

I hug my arms and check the small digiclock on the bedside stand. Just after seven.

The Enactment Office wanted me there by eight. If I don't show, they might send people. Those people might see Dad.

And pass along the info to the Records Officials.

Hell.

I bolt for the shower. Fifteen minutes later, I'm dripping, dressed, and beside the couch. I touch Dad's shoulder, but he doesn't move. I shake him.

"Mmmhmm," he mumbles.

"There's Berrimix in the cabinet, some milk, and some juice. Use the bathroom over there." I point to the door opposite the bedroom's. "If you go into my room, I'll kill you."

He flaps a hand at me and snuggles deeper into the couch.

I scan the suite. No spare keypasses or money lying around, no trinkets worth pawning. I scrabble into my shoes and run out the door.

"MS. FRANKS." AN OLDER WOMAN IN A DEEP BLUE SUIT materializes at my elbow before I can follow the revolving door back outside.

The skytower lobby stretches in windows and reflections. Mirrored floor and ceiling tiles refracting an infinite number of Kits, all stepping in unison. I face front, but they crowd my peripheral until I'm a feedshow of jitters.

The woman walks us past the central oval desk to the lone door beyond. The desk sentry doesn't look up from his digislate, but I'd bet a week's worth of reds he's counting my steps in the mirrors.

At least I'm not into skirts, else he'd have something to see.

The woman flattens her hand against the lone silver door and the circuits underneath blossom into threads of light. The door splits down the middle. She gestures me into a flat gray hall. "Thank you for your prompt arrival. We appreciate punctuality."

I was five minutes late.

"Anytime," I say.

Our strides sync, and I keep my eyes on the floor. It's also silver, no mirrors or seams. No seams in my companion, either, her suit a second skin. Probably custom made. Lordling attire. Or maybe Investigative Enactors get paid more than their City counterparts.

The woman stops midway to nowhere in front of a door that looks exactly like all the others. Her palm presses its center, and it opens on a blank white room with a table, two chairs, and nothing else. Smooth walls, smooth floor, smooth ceiling.

"Have a seat," she says.

I step inside and something whooshes behind me, almost a breeze. I turn. The door's closed. More than that, it's *gone*. I spread my hands over the wall, but there's nothing. No telltale seams scrape my fingers, no subsurface circuits light up. The entry wall remains as blank as the other three.

I'm trapped in a box in the Investigative Enactment Office and no one knows I'm here.

I knock my forehead against the wall. It's cool, smooth, and full of eyes. I can feel them, every last camera I can't see.

Just like I can't see the door.

I push off the wall and sink into a chair like a good little detainee. Fold my nonthreatening hands on the empty table and let the seconds tick into minutes. Lots of minutes.

No one comes.

Which means I'm somebody's latest sideshow. I drum my fingers against my wrist to give them something to see.

Yonni would always tap her fingers while waiting. Given half a second of downtime, she'd be sounding out the rhythm of some old song against doorframes or counter-tops. By contrast Mom's hands were always still as stone.

The tapping must get someone's attention. The wall cracks open and a man steps through. Brown hair, sharp eyes, broad shoulders. He's reassurance and rough grace, sleek but not too sleek. Familiar somehow—he carries himself like Dad does, when Dad's sober and on his game— but that's not it. Not the right correlation. But he reminds me of *someone.*

"Ms. Franks," he says.

"Present," I say.

The door slides shut.

He takes the chair opposite. I straighten and drop my hands to my lap. The room's general whiteness washes out his skin. His blue-black suit overcompensates, gives him form.

The man takes my measure and doesn't comment, not even with his eyes. "Tell me about the Accounting."

Have you ever seen the future, Kit?

I don't move, don't blink.

Premonitions. Yonni was into premonitions. She was into dreams, too—would sometimes accept or refuse clients by them. A dream's the reason she first went out with Missa, who became her last lover, the only one where "love" applied. After Missa, there was never anyone else.

Have you ever had a moment, where without any evidence whatsoever, you just knew?

This man could happily kill me at breakfast, then forget I existed by lunch.

I relax into my seat. Whatever happens here won't give anyone nightmares, least of all him. "Accounts? Like money? Looking for a loan?"

The man doesn't move. "Did your mother mention it?"

"A loan? From me? She worked at the Archive. She probably made more than you."

His eyebrow lifts. A pale bow over shallow sockets, the perfect, unstated, *wanna bet?* But his voice remains neutral. "Tell me about the Accounting."

"I think it has to do with numbers, but you know, I dropped out of school."

He smiles. A twisted snake of a thing that bites my gut. The hairs on my neck try to scramble for safety, but safety isn't what this is about.

"Ms. Franks," he says, moderate, relaxed. "I am certain I don't need to remind you of the severity of your situation."

I smile right back. "That assumes the situation trumps the people involved. 'Beware no one more than yourself, for we carry our worst enemies within.'"

Yonni always hated it when I quoted Gilken at her.

The suit doesn't even blink. "You're saying you are your

41

own worst enemy, Ms. Franks?"

"I'm saying I'm scarier than you."

He doesn't move a muscle—the patient, professional Adult.

Until his mouth opens, and his voice dips into I-will-skin-you territory. "I very much doubt it."

This is almost fun. "I don't."

He leans forward at speed, his presence a near physical weight. I want to hunch over, curl up, slam a dozen doors between me and him.

I set my jaw and don't.

"There are other methods to ensure cooperation," he says.

And likely none of them are quick. This is not a man who gets nightmares.

What the hell am I doing?

I cross my arms. "Mom took off when I was eight." True. "She only walked into my life a month back." Also true, for a given value of truth. "What do you think I know?"

The room seems to shift with each word. The question was stupid, but the truth is a disaster. He owns the field now. It's in his eyes, in the prickled bite under my skin.

"Why don't we do a mind map and find out?" he says.

My jaw drops.

Mind maps involve steel chairs and wires and jacking

with one's head. Long needles, maybe drills. It was all over the newsfeeds last year, the debate over continued experimentation—if the minimal-at-best information garnered was worth leaving the subject a drooling puppet. The universal consensus was no.

"It's illegal," I say.

"It's regulated," he counters. "I'll have the room set up in an hour."

A room. I mouth the word, roll the *o*'s on my tongue. They squiggle and bounce and solve everything. I laugh, rocking my chair back on its legs.

Drooling puppet. Not my first choice, but good as any.

I lean forward, slam my palms on the table, and mirror his dead-eyed stare. "Okay, then. Map me."

His eyes flash. Shock? Anger? Less than a second and more than enough. He wants something, which means he has something to lose.

I don't.

Match, set, game.

He rises without a word. Steps to the wall, does the palm bit, and slips through.

I stretch and lock my hands behind my head.

I won't even have to do anything. They'll take care of it all for me. No one will have to find the body and mop me up. No one will see me and think Mom.

"Ms. Franks?" My earlier escort appears. "If you would follow me."

I hop up and march.

Her steps are brisk but less demanding than before. She doesn't take my arm or match my pace or wait for me. She scans her palm at the end of the hall, and the door opens to . . . the lobby? Big desk, bored sentry, mirror self-propagating eternities.

"So the mapping's in another facility?" I ask.

The woman doesn't slow down. She glides across the mirrors and opens the skinny door beside the revolving one. She waits, expressionless, as I step through.

"Where to?" I ask.

"Your choice, Ms. Franks," she says and shuts the door.

THEY WERE SUPPOSED TO MAP ME.

I push out onto the rooftop of the Gilken Museum with enough force that the door rebounds off the wall. No one's bothered to change the entry codes yet, and if they had I'd pop the locks. The museum isn't highly secure or populated mid-morning or even in general. No one saw me slip in. No one was around. No one is ever around. I used to borrow one of the inventory digislates with general network access, then slip up here to research. It started with Yonni's meds, finding her new ones, then after—

After I just wanted off-planet. The scholarship would have paid for everything. I'd be somewhere else, *someone* else.

Guess I did manage to pull that last one off. I'm the hack-bomber's daughter. Dreams do come true.

I kick off my shoes and start across the roof.

"*You* again," someone says.

I slam to a halt, fists clenched and eyes tight.

You've got to be kidding me.

But no, there he is—that same power technician, barrel arms jammed deep in the innards of an open fuse box. Sweat slicked, sun drenched, and glaring my death.

Here he was, just trying to work, and now he has to deal with my sorry self.

He pulls his hands free. "What the hell are you—?"

I turn right back around and walk out.

THEN

WALK HOME BAREFOOT. AGAIN. AS IF I HAVE END-less shoes to strew about.

My heels hurt. The pavement is hot and dusty, and every time I curl my toes something catches in the crease. Rocks, old wrappers, glass.

I could have been halfway to crazy by now, tied to a chair with a needle in my brain. It wouldn't hurt. They'd numb me from the inside out, and I'd wake up different.

Or not at all.

Mom worked with the Archive's mind mapping research division for a stretch, before switching to scent mapping instead. She explained it once, over coffee. How scents could be used to trigger reactions in people or objects on a fundamental level, and how the effect could be directed and magnified with the help of an implanted receptor. She talked for an hour while the coffee got cold and people wandered in and out of the café without sparing us a glance. A month ago, she was an Archivest and I was a tour guide, and everyone could care less. I watched them instead of her.

Until Mom cut herself off midsentence. *Just say it.*

Say what? I asked.

That you hate me.

I took my mug with both hands to keep them still. *I'd have to know you to hate you,* I said.

A long, long silence.

I can fix that, she said.

I thought she meant she was going to stick around long enough for me to get to know her. Stupid.

The midday sun bakes the city gold before South Central finally bleeds into West 1st and I'm almost home.

"I'm telling you, Ricky," screams a distant, Dee-like voice, "you better damn well open this door!"

No. Oh no. Dad can't have answered the visitor intercom. He couldn't be that stupid.

I sprint the rest of the block and swing left onto my street.

Dee stands at the entrance to my tower, lips pressed to the intercom box beside the keypass scanner, her finger stiff on the button. "What the hell are you doing in my apartment?"

"Kit's apartment," Dad responds through the scratchy speaker. "And I'm visiting my daughter."

Yep. Dad is definitely that stupid.

My legs fold and I land on my butt on the curb. My feet feel every hour I've walked, and one of my toes trickles blood.

Four floors up, a woman with a hair-frizzed halo sticks her head out a window. "God dammit, leave the man alone," she calls. "He wants to visit his kid, let him visit his kid."

"Thank you," says Dad. "Finally."

Dee backs up to yell at the stranger. "You mean the kid he ditched when she was seven?"

"Nine!" Dad blares righteous indignation. "Millie was gone, and I was going to come back. I was on a job."

"Oh, really? You mean one with two legs and tits?"

Two more windows shoot up on levels one and three. Mrs. Divs pops her wrinkled head out of the lowest one. "You do not talk like that outside my front door, young missy. You get off my steps or I'm calling the Enactors."

Great. There goes my suite.

"Excuse me, we're having a private conversation," Dee snaps.

A young guy hangs out of the window higher up. "Then maybe you should have it where we all can't hear you."

"And maybe you should get your big fat—"

"Okay," I yell, hauling myself to my feet. "Okay, show's over. Everybody back up."

Mrs. Divs swings her shaky finger at me. "Kit?"

"Kit?" echoes Dad from the speakers. "Dee's here! Did you see—"

"Where the hell have you been?" Dee asks.

"What's it matter?" I crest the steps and press the intercom button. "Shut up, Dad."

"You bet it matters," Dee says. "Here you are, prancing around while Greg—"

"Kit?" Mrs. Divs asks, louder.

"Go on back inside, Mrs. Divs," I call, leaning past Dee's shoulder. "I've got this."

Big mistake. Dee grabs my shirt and shoves me, hard, into the wall. My head bounces—cracks?—and the world blurs.

Dee shakes me in the recoil until the world bleeds color. "Greg's facing lockdown, and you let Ricky in? *Him?*"

"Dammit, Dee." I try to push her off, but there's thunder in my brain. "Greg's always facing lockdown."

"You unhand her!" Mrs. Divs shouts. "You unhand her right now!"

"It's okay, Mrs. Divs," I say. "Just go back inside."

"You call this okay?" Dee rears and backhands me. My cheek grates between my teeth. "If I lose Greg because of you, I swear to God—"

Her hand swoops for a second strike, then stops mid-air. I can read the lines in her palm. They say she's going to hit me.

Except she doesn't. Someone's grabbed her wrist. A larger hand, a guy's hand. The one from upstairs?

"Here's a bet for you." He has a cheerful voice, not loud or angry. He maneuvers Dee back without exactly pushing, and plants himself firmly between her and me. Lots of dark hair, bare shoulders, and neck. "How long will you last when your opponent fights back?"

Dee doesn't miss a beat, her words for me alone. "Taking after Mom, are we? Got yourself a new toy?"

"Don't." I slide past the guy and almost fall over. Almost. "Don't even."

Mrs. Divs appears in the doorway, waving her cane like a damn laserblade. "Be gone, wretch! If you think I tolerate this kind of behavior on my doorstep—"

Dee reaches to yank it from her hand, but I'm there first and all she gets is my hair. I plant myself in the doorway.

"Don't you get in the middle of my altercation!" Mrs. Divs thumps me in the back, for all the good it does her.

I've found my feet and I don't budge.

The guy moves closer to retake the role of buffer, but I hold up my hand. This isn't his fight or Mrs. Divs's.

"I'm the oldest!" Dee yells. "Me! That suite belongs to me. Not you, and sure as hell not Ricky."

Her spit flecks my cheek and lips. Sticky little slugs I'll lose face by wiping off.

As if she, of all people, has a *right*.

I meet her eyes, search for a soul to eviscerate. "You want to talk about why you got cut out? Because trust me, Dee, I'm game."

51

She steps back, almost jerks. Some things we don't talk about. Ever. The agreement so tactile it could be written in blood.

Dee might consider screwing Yonni over fair game, but Greg stopping by Missa's sick room? When Missa was dying and Yonni held her hand through every treatment, sleeping in the Medicenter then later at Missa's cloudsuite when there was nothing left to do? When Greg came over to "offer support" and then disappeared with Missa's last med pack so she died in pain? Because by the time I realized and tracked his sorry ass down and got some of them back, it was already too late.

One of those things.

Missa was a lordling. Nobody steals from lordlings, not even the pawn dealers of East 5th. Enactors have priorities, and lordlings are it.

Dee doesn't blink, lips curving a rebuttal.

My fists squeeze so hard they hurt and I commit familial suicide.

"Mrs. Divs," I say. "Why don't you go ahead and call those Enactors. We can have a nice, long conversation."

Dee freezes. Takes a beat for her mouth to work. "You wouldn't."

I smile. "Watch me."

"Kit?" asks Mrs. Divs, uncertain.

"No." Dee shakes her head. "You wouldn't. You wouldn't dare."

"Really? Whose daughter am I?"

All her light drains, her fight, her assurance.

There's no arguing that.

I jerk my head for her to leave, and she does. No argument, no threat, shoulders almost hunched.

If the Enactors ever discovered Greg stole from a lordling—not to mention *what* he stole, highly regulated and otherwise illegal pain meds—that'd be it. The end of Greg.

Dee doesn't look back as she walks down the street. She doesn't run, but every stuttered step says she wants to.

Dee never runs from anything.

Whose daughter am I?

Mom's.

I hug my arms and stare at nothing.

"Kit?" A soft touch on my shoulder. It's the guy. He has thick mop-like hair, wide lips, and narrow, relaxed eyes that arc. At least, what I can see of them under his bangs.

The guy from the market, yesterday, lunch, who stares into fans and upturns tables.

"You?" I ask.

His mouth promises way more smile then it gives, a soft tug followed by a wink. "Always a pleasure."

What the hell?

I shrug him off. "How do you know my name?"

"You mean, apart from the screaming?" he asks. "That feed special."

Was there anyone in this city who was away from their screens that day?

"Yes. Right." I dig my fingers into the bridge of my nose and call up to whatever windows are still open, "Okay, show's over. Back to your regular newscasts."

A tissuey hand slips around my arm. Mrs. Divs. "You poor dear, what awful relatives you have. Come in and sit." She tugs me into the lobby, toward the hall and her suite. Mop-head follows, closing the main door behind us.

"Thanks, Mrs. Divs, but I should get home."

"Why? Your father's up there."

Hell. She's right.

"I thought your gran didn't want him in her place. Didn't she make a will or something?" Mrs. Divs's cane thuds heavy on the carpet, though she leans mostly on me.

One call to the Records Office and Mrs. Divs could get me evicted.

"Or something," I say.

The guy sidles close, listening in. As if I need anyone else having power over me and my place. Not that Yonni said Dad couldn't enter the suite, but she did state he couldn't stay overnight.

With any luck, no one heard him come in yesterday.

Yeah, and the sun revolves around the moon.

Mrs. Divs pushes open her door. "Come on in, now. You, too, Niles."

Of course Mrs. Divs knows him. She knows everyone in the building. Probably keeps mental files of our birth dates, Record IDs, and what we last ate for breakfast.

The name suits him. Maybe it's the bangs. They slope.

He has to be recent, I don't remember him moving in. Or the woman who stuck up for Dad, come to that.

Niles meets my assessment and winks. Again.

Something's up.

Mrs. Divs lives in spotless lace. White webs cover her lone window, the rickety side tables, and the back of her couch. Even the wall-screen with its muted newscast is lace strewn. Her furniture matches, carved legs and floral cushions worn but cared for. Must have cost a mint at one time.

A big green jar gleams on the closest side table. Yonni moved us here when I was twelve, and while most of the world has shrunk as I've grown, Mrs. Divs's cookie jar remains fat as ever.

She catches me looking. "Go on, then. Get Niles one, too. I'll make tea."

She taps off into the kitchen. I pounce on the jar. Remove the lid with slow care and sniff. Sugar, lots of sugar, dried whitepips, and . . . pacanuts? I reach in and pull out a frosted star. Bright teal. She even dyed the dough to match. The teals are best.

I offer it to Niles.

He shakes his head. "Not a fan of cookies."

"In general, or hers specifically?"

He drops onto the couch. "General. Too crunchy."

"These aren't." I toss him the cookie and get my own—a pink moon so deep it's almost red.

Niles commands the couch with an elbow thrown over the back and legs askew. A crumpled mess of limbs and hair. Mrs. Divs's furniture was once pricey, but she hasn't much of it. Seating consists of the couch.

Niles must catch on, because he folds himself up against one corner. Back straight, legs crossed. Demure, even. Until he tosses out that half-there smile and pats the cushion next to him.

"What was yesterday about?" I ask.

He shrugs, unfazed. "Looked like you could use a hand."

I didn't. I was fine.

"Were you watching me?" I ask.

He gives me a long, slow once-over, until I can't fight the blood in my cheeks. "What if I was?"

And I gave this guy a cookie.

"Gawking at the murderer's daughter?"

It's his turn to blush, the carpet suddenly fascinating. "No."

Whatever.

I lean against the door and watch the screen. Pristine newscasters mouth silent opinions before cutting to Lady Galton in all her blonde ringlet glory. She's the only person I've ever seen, on-screen or off-, who can wear ruffles and still project power. That lace hides teeth. The captions reiterate what she's been saying since the Lord's death. It's fine, we're all fine, the Prime assures her he's doing his best to find the next House Heir—despite his continued lack of success. As the head of the Enactors, the Prime has endless resources at his disposal, so there must be excellent reasons as to *why* he hasn't found the Heir already—but regardless we can rest assured our Acting Lady, as our late Lord's beloved wife, will see our House safely through this terrible crisis.

Of course she will.

Niles eyes me from the couch. "You know, I don't bite."

"So I've noticed." I glance at the cookie he hasn't touched. Such a waste of sugar.

He grins and tosses the cookie back to me. Perfect trajectory, I barely have to move to catch it.

"All yours," he says.

Mrs. Divs returns, balancing a tray. Niles hops up and takes it from her, laying the tray on the low central table.

She beams and sits on one end of the couch, tugging the tray closer. The steam from the teapot dances.

"Don't you be glaring at us from on high, girl," Mrs. Divs says. "Sit."

Niles grins. With Mrs. Divs in the corner, whenever I sit he'll be right beside me. Lucky him, I'm sweaty as hell. And grimy. And probably bleeding everywhere.

Oh hell.

I lift a foot—which really aches, thinking about it—to find red-brown streaks smeared deep in the rug. It's a nice rug, with flowers and swirls. Probably the only rug in the building worth *not* getting blood on.

So, of course, I walk all over it.

My breath stops. Cuts out. Smothered by the mountain in my chest that rises like a flightwing and cracks every thought into one.

They should have just mapped me. Or the power tech should have taken the day off.

My legs shake and I'll be on my knees bleeding on the carpet if I don't calm down.

Breathe, Kit. Come on, breathe.

"Kit," warns Mrs. Divs, "I don't see you sitting."

Air rushes in and I gasp.

"You okay?" Niles is at my elbow, not reaching or touching, scanning me over. "Wow, your feet are—"

"Fine," I snap, turning to Mrs. Divs. "I've ruined your rug. I'll fix it."

Just don't ask me how.

"Oh, you mean the blood? Don't go getting all in a fuss, there are ways and means. Now you get your butt on this couch." She pats the cushion beside her while offering the evil eye, Niles bites his lip, and there's nothing for it but to tiptoe over and collapse as ordered.

The fluffy cushions swallow me in, then bounce as Niles takes the last spot.

"What ways and means specifically?" asks Niles.

"Never you mind." Mrs. Divs bats pale lashes, pours tea, and hands the first cup to him.

He accepts with reverence, batting his own much darker lashes, which are also, of course, long.

"I see you rolling your eyes, young lady," says Mrs. Divs.

I wasn't. Visibly.

My teacup arrives with her prim sniff.

"Now, Kit, I know family can sometimes be quite beyond our control, but fighting over intercoms? Causing a ruckus in the middle of the street? One would think we lived on the Brink."

I balance my feet off the floor and try not to bleed on anything. "I'll handle it."

"I know Yonni's passing was . . . difficult, and then this

unfortunate incident with your mother, but that is no excuse to throw good conduct after bad. Yonni would be absolutely horrified to know you let that man spend the night in her place after he showed up wasted on the doorstep—don't think I didn't see that."

She's right. Yonni would skin me. Her last conversation with Dad involved screaming and a slap that sent Dad reeling. *A month. My grandbaby was alone a month while you weren't even on the same damn planet. How the* hell *are you my child?*

The first and last time I saw her strike anyone, heard that level of ice in her voice. She refused him entry last time he stopped by, and now he's sleeping on her couch.

I set the tea on the table, not thirsty anymore.

"You shouldn't have let him in," says Mrs. Divs. "It was very bad of you—and now this with your intolerable aunt. Yonni always said her children were tyrants, but I never heard a peep from them all the time she was here. She managed them with a steel fist and that is what you must do." She balls her wrinkled fingers and holds them up high. "Steel."

Apparently, blackmailing Dee with my cousin's freedom isn't ruthless enough.

The cookies join the tea on the table. Sugar sticks to my palms, gritty crumbles wedged between shaking fingers. I flatten them on my thighs.

"You can do it, dear." Mrs. Divs squeezes my shoulder. "Now that that's all settled, I think it's about time you dyed your hair."

Wait, what?

She folds her hands with a lordling's authority and nods once. I rewind the last few seconds in my head and come up blank. Niles looks equally mystified, eyebrows knit and fingers tapping his knee as if counting out the replay. I catch his eye, but he shrugs in a *don't look at me*.

"My hair?" I ask.

"Of course, dear." Mrs. Divs clucks and shakes her head. "Niles, be a dear and go grab the box on my bed, would you? I pulled it from the closet last night. My room's just down the hall." Niles hops to and disappears down the hall past the kitchen and returns a minute later, box in hand. At Mrs. Divs's nod, he gives it to me.

I lift the hinged lid. Colorkits, a mess of them. Pretty men and women with vibrant locks. One particular redhead winks above a scrawled *Sunset Luminance* in curly font.

"You're quite distinctive, you know," says Mrs. Divs, "just like . . . well. What with that feedshow special, it might be a good idea not to look quite so distinctive, if you take my meaning." She pats my knee. "You'd be quite fetching as a blonde or a redhead. Niles agrees, don't you, Niles?"

He pockets his hands and literally distances himself

from the conversation—a full step back. "I . . . defer to your judgment."

"That means 'no,'" I say.

Mrs. Divs shrugs this off. "He's just being shy."

"Shy?" asks Niles.

That's one word for it.

"Thanks, Mrs. Divs, but I don't even know how to use these." I replace the lid and push the box away.

She pushes it right back. "It's easy, there's a booklet. Do this tonight, and tomorrow you'll—how does it go?—*be a new soul for the new year.*"

"But we're midyear," says Niles.

I pause, hand hovering short of a second push. Everyone always mixes up that quote, and that's not what Gilken meant. Not entirely. "'The object of the new year isn't that we have a new year. It's that we are new souls, with fresh backbones, ears, and eyes. Unless we understand how to start afresh, we'll never be effective.'"

Mrs. Divs sips her tea. "Ah yes, that was it."

My eyes narrow. Gilken has many popular quotes, but that's not one of them. "You planned that."

"I've no idea what you mean," she says, "though it is nice to know the younger generation still respects our Archive's founder. Such a beautiful sentiment, is it not? Reinvention to improve effectiveness." She bunches her fingers. "Fists of steel, dear. Fists of steel. This, dear, is your new soul."

All sealed up in a prepackaged box.

Two steps into the outer entrance hall, after the telltale click of Mrs. Divs's door, Niles snags the colorkit box from my hands. He stuffs it under one arm and walks backward toward the elevator. "Walk you home."

"I think I can make it." I reach for the box, but he holds it out of reach. He has only an inch on me, maybe two, but he more than makes up for it in arm length. I bounce, reach, and miss by inches. He's fast.

And I'm done.

"Fine, knock yourself out." I duck around him to the stairs.

"Hey!" He reaches the stairwell door before I do, props it open with his back. "Don't be like that."

"And what should I be like? You have that all figured out?"

He blinks, leaning back into the door until the handle hits the wall. I move past him to the stairs.

"Wait." He straightens, brushing off his tank and slacks as if shedding a second skin. Swaps the box between arms and holds out his hand as if we're at some kind of fancy party. "Wasn't trying to get off on the wrong foot. I'm Niles."

"And I'm the hack-bomber's daughter." I ignore his hand but he doesn't drop it.

If anything, he reaches closer. "Kit, right?"

"Fine." I take his hand and do the whole nice-to-meet-you bit. His fingers are cool. "Yes, Kit. Can I have the color boxes now?"

He smiles, a habit apparently. "Then what excuse would I have to walk you home?"

I drop his hand and hit the stairs. Three steps and he's beside me again. "So, how are your feet?"

"None of your business."

"Are you bleeding anywhere else?"

"Why do you care?"

"Just making conversation."

"Don't."

He shrugs, unfazed. "All right."

People are weird.

He winks. We climb. A clatter of echoes and silence. After the first two landings, the day catches up with claws and my feet drag, each harder to lift. Setting them down doesn't feel too great, either. We clear the third floor.

"What was with the other day?" I ask.

"Hmm?"

"At the Market. You flipped the table on purpose."

He shrugs. "Nah, just clumsy."

I stop. Two steps up, so does he. We stare.

"Cut the act," I say.

"Act?"

"Charm, whatever. What was up with yesterday?"

Another shift of arms and shoulders, the box sliding from one hand to another, back and forth. Once, twice, stop. "Answer me something."

"I asked first."

He looks at me, into me, a straight up visual lock. "Why didn't you jump?"

I freeze, the air taut with webs and spiders, and a stare I can't break without letting him win. "What?"

"On the walkway, above the fans." Objective and neutral, like asking about the weather. Even his body language has nothing to say. "That's what you were up there for, right? You thought about it."

He's dreaming this up, he was too far away to see.

He should have been too far away to see.

My arms half reach to hug my chest. I force them to my sides. "You don't know what I was thinking."

His brows flatline in a *yeah, right*. "It'd be an ugly way to die."

Which was the problem.

"Do I look dead?" I jump the next three steps, landing on the one past his, and take the rest two at a time.

This is not a conversation I'm having, least of all with him.

He keeps up, reaching my landing just as I hit the door. "Are you okay?"

He sounds so sincere, even honest, and I laugh. "Is this a trick question?"

Which apparently is the key to pissing him off.

"Fine." He steps closer, knuckles shiny on the box. "Are you going to try again?"

"What's it to you?"

The air vibrates and me with it, feeding the tension or reflecting it back.

"Because I *know*," he says. "Which means not stopping you is as bad as pushing you myself."

"You want the chance? Then have at it." I grab the stairwell rail with both hands. We're only five stories up, so not guaranteed lethal, but with any luck I'll break my neck on the way down. I plant a bare foot on the central pipe and hoist myself up. I've barely cleared the bar when arms wrap my waist and *haul*. We stumble and almost crash, his back hitting the wall and mine his chest. But we're still on the landing, still stable.

Except now he's squeezing me like the world might end if he lets go.

"What the hell?" he whispers, ragged in the quiet. Everything is ragged; our breath, my heart.

"You almost—" he swears, forehead falling to my skull as

he swears again.

I know that tone, this hold, that swear. Terror. Fully formed and nothing but. He's rife with it, the echoes burning through his hands and chest—leaking out and into me. My stomach knots heavy and breathing hurts.

I almost broke him. Scraping me off the stairwell floor probably would have. Seeing me fall, all that blood.

Just like I broke Dee. She retreated. Dee never retreats.

At least Mom killed people outright. Apparently I have other ways.

I curl forward.

"No." Niles pulls me close, but my legs aren't stable. Without the wall, neither are his. We sink. The floor's cold. The colorkit box lies close by.

We sit. His grip doesn't ease, like he thinks I'll try again.

He's right. Wrong? I don't know anymore.

"It's all right," I say.

"No, it's damn well not—"

"I won't do anything here."

"So it'll be somewhere else?"

"I . . ."

Maybe? Probably? I don't know.

"God," he says.

"It's not on your head," I say. "I'm not on your head."

"You have no idea." He sighs and knocks back against the wall.

I pull away to look at him, and his arms finally ease up. "I didn't ask you to see me. I don't *know* you."

His eyes are dark and shuttered and close when I look too long. Without them open, he loses years and gains exhaustion. "Promise me something?"

But that's more than I can give. "I can't—"

"Not tonight." He blinks, tries for a smile. It doesn't last. "Just not tonight."

As if I could. Today's courage died when he hauled me back. Or else when the Enactor walked me to freedom.

They should have just mapped me.

"Okay." I disentangle and climb to my feet. The stairwell is stuffy as hell and I'm freezing, at least in the places his arms just were.

He stands as I retrieve the colorkits. "Promise." Not a question.

"Fine," I say. "Promise."

I UNLOCK THE DOOR TO THE BLARE OF THE NEWS-feeds. Dad has my small wall-screen jacked up to full volume. Some digislate ad. My neighbors probably hate me.

Not that this is half as loud as the earlier show outside.

He's also lit a mass of air-freshener sticks, which smoke a tangled web of scents from the kitchen counter.

"Kit? That you?" Dad calls from the couch.

"Yeah." I back-kick the door closed. "Turn it down, Dad. The whole building can hear."

He half straightens from his slouch to dig up the screen remote, hitting mute just as a newscast switches on. Same one Mrs. Divs had running, full of sleek professionals with practiced smiles.

"Where you been, doll?" He leans up, kisses my cheek, sloppy and wet. He used to do that, hand out kisses, back when he, Mom, and I were something of a unit. Known as a family, even seen in each other's company. He would sometimes buy me ices; Mom would sometimes braid my hair.

Then Dad started bringing over people who weren't Mom, and swore me not to tell. He'd smile when I promised.

He's smiling now.

"How did Dee know you were here?" I ask.

He shrugs. "She called while you were out. I didn't know who it was."

"Then you shouldn't have answered," I say.

"But what if it was you?" He sinks into the couch, retrieves a flask from some hidden pocket and stares at the newsfeed. "You've been gone all day, what if you needed me?"

I needed him when I was nine.

"You're leaving tomorrow," I say.

He looks up, face open, eyes huge. "Kit—"

"Dad." Yonni's tone, a warning.

He sighs, reaching up to rub my hip. "We'll talk about it tomorrow."

I don't want to talk about it tomorrow. I don't want to talk about it now.

On-screen, the newscasters have switched to a new interview feed. Not Lady Galton this time, but a man. Brown-haired, sharp-eyed, and without being blatant.

The Enactor from the interview room.

A red caption floats below: *Prime*.

The Prime? I was interrogated by the freakin' *Prime*? The man who controls the Enactors. The only House Official with almost bloodling-level power, without actually being a bloodling. I might as well have been questioned by Lady Galton, or Lord Galton's ghost.

My chest empties, and I sink into the couch beside Dad.

The Prime doesn't play to the cameras, like the Lady, and it's not like I memorized his face. Why would I? I'd have as much chance of running into him as I would a bloodling—or a lordling come to that, with the exception of Missa.

The Prime wants to map me.

I curl over the colorkit box—now in my lap, I didn't drop it—and proceed not to feel. Anything. Like a heartbeat.

The Prime knows about the Accounting.

Which means it's real.

"Kit?" Dad scoots close and rubs my back. "What's up, baby doll?"

I shake my head. There's no air in the room and too much under my skin.

What's up, baby? Dad asked, leaning over Mom's shoulder as she sat at the kitchen table and built algorithms on her digislate. She could always make the numbers dance, and the letters, and the little symbols in between. I sat one chair over with my sandwich and juice, little hand sticky from both.

Mom didn't lift her head or slow her fingers. *Years, it'd take years. The prep alone, the focus—it'd be this, it could only be this.*

She'd said that before that night, more than once, to herself and to me.

This what? Dad asked.

She paused, looked up, her smile a slow incredible thing. *The Accounting. I've cracked it.*

"Baby?" Dad brushes my hair off my temple and gently

raps my skull with his knuckles. "Hey, you still in there?"

I yank away from his hand, the couch.

From Mom at the table and me with my sandwich. From the beauty of her grin.

"Kit?" Dad asks.

That's wonderful, baby! he'd said.

Mom turned serious. *I'd have to dedicate everything to it; there could be nothing else.*

He rubbed her neck. *You do what you need to.*

Thank you, Ricky, she'd said, and disappeared the next day. No note, no goodbye. One day she was there, and the next she wasn't.

He reaches for me. "Don't block the screen, baby. Here, sit—"

"Watch your show, Dad." I bolt into my bedroom and lock the door. I dump the colorkits on the bed and lock myself in the bathroom. It's tiny, with a box shower and scuffed white tiles, though larger than the half bath off the living room. But the real difference between them is the mirror. Yonni splurged on the mirror. It stretches from wall to ceiling, rimmed in woven tube lights that glow orange.

I'm orange. Cheek swollen. Lip puffed but not quite busted. Hair frizzed, shirt sweat-streaked and a little askew. I might have been in a fight, or three. But under it all, despite the mess and the tangles, I'm still Mom.

Heart-edged jaw, sharp nose, jet hair. Mom was never unkempt, never not perfect, and still—still, I'm her.

No wonder the Prime wanted to map me. Except he didn't. Maybe he thinks it too risky, that my brain would break before he extracted whatever he thinks I know.

Tell me about the Accounting.

Vengeance. Simple as that.

The late Lord Galton gutted the independent planets. Seized, evacuated, and/or killed every living soul there in order to split the planet and suck energy from its core. They never stood a chance, not against the force of our House. He destroyed their homes to fuel ours.

Mom was from one of those independents, born and raised there until she was seven or nine. She wasn't the only survivor, and she'd meet with the others at night sometimes, when I was in bed or supposed to be. They had two refrains: *Galton must be held to Account* and *They will know our loss.*

I tug my hair out of its ponytail and comb my fingers through. It falls to my elbows, unremittent black. Just like hers.

"'Unless we understand how to start afresh,'" I quote, soft, "'we'll never be effective. Unless we begin as if we've never existed before, we'll never exist afterward.'"

I stare at the Mom in the mirror.

"You don't exist, but I will."

THE COLORKIT DOESN'T DO ANYTHING.

The guy on the front of Sunset Luminescence beckons from under vibrant mahogany, but my black hair is still black. The mirror fogs as I lean close, my scalp a ropy, damp mass. Maybe a bit orange, but in these lights everything's orange.

I sort through the colorkit's used gloves and tubes for the included digisheet—a thin, flimsy screen smeared from my fingerprints. Its glossy text reads, *after thirty minutes, rinse the color and prepare for the new you.*

"I don't get it," I say, but disposable digisheets aren't programmed to answer questions.

Perhaps my hair is too dark for this. I need something lighter.

I retrieve Mrs. Divs's box from the bed and dig through shades of red and blonde. One girl's head is pure white, skin nearly light enough to match. *Ghostfire*—a dye and lightening treatment. Sounds right. I dump the contents on the counter, unscrew the tube labeled #1 and dump the contents on my head. Cold, slimy goo slinks everywhere—in my ear, down my neck, on my shirt. I tap the digisheet for the process time.

One hour. I have to stand here and drip for an hour. I screw up Yonni's bedroom carpet and she'll return from the grave to gut me.

Nothing else for it. I strip out of my clothes, fill the sink with water, and soak my shirt. Might as well salvage something. Then I slide back the opaque glass door to the shower and step inside. It's tiny—I have to pull my knees up to my chin in order to sit—but safe. Even I can't ruin EverClean tile. This stuff would stand up to acid.

I close my eyes and wait.

BUZZZIT, BUZZZIT.

The flipcom won't stop. High vibrations with cracked ends. My neck cramps, my back hurts, and my butt sticks to the tile.

Shower tile. I fell asleep.

The flipcom falls silent for three full seconds, then starts again.

No one ever calls twice in a row—unless Greg's got himself in city lockup. He has this thing about not asking Dee to bail him out, something about pride, which somehow doesn't extend to me.

Buzzzit.

I de-stick myself from the floor and crawl out of the shower. Dig through my discarded clothes for the flipcom, and press it to my ear. "What?"

"Franks?" asks the phone voice, confused but fast on the ball.

Not Greg, then.

"Yeah?"

"It's Jallon Remmings." My former boss, official head of the Gilken Museum.

The man who fired me.

I grab my shirt and cover myself up. "Mr. Remmings."

He coughs, clears his throat. The silence stretches and he coughs again. I don't know what he's hoping for, but I'm not about to fill in.

"We've missed you on the rotation," he says.

"I thought I was a detriment."

That's what he'd said, a detriment. The daughter of a murderer. *You understand why I can't keep you on.*

"No, no," Mr. Remmings says. "Not you, yourself, merely your connections."

"I thought there wasn't a difference."

He doesn't pause. "Would you be available to come on shift tomorrow? Early?"

I run the words through my head twice over and still come up blank.

"What?" I ask.

He sighs. "I've no one to take the shift. Joan is out sick, Henri has a family event, and Denze is still mastering tour-level knowledge."

Denze Remmings, a nephew, has three years of tour-level knowledge pounded into his skull. It's amazing the detail of random Gilken info he can dish out when a bet's on. Even more amazing is how it all evaporates the moment work might be involved. If you need a hand, you count on Denze to be somewhere else.

"So you're letting Millie Oen's daughter back in?"

His voice creaks, as if the words are hard to pull. "You are not your mother."

"And you have no one to cover the shift."

The silence of admission.

"So you're giving me my job back," I say.

Another pause. "Potentially. You'll have the day's wage. If all goes well, we can discuss it further."

Which isn't a yes, but it's something.

I won't be able to cover power for the suite without work for long, little less buy food. And it's not like anyone else will hire me.

"You'll be here tomorrow?" Mr. Remmings asks.

"I'll be there."

"Good," he says and hangs up.

I stare at the flipcom.

A job. I have my job. Possibly.

My whole body exhales, and I lean into the shower door. My head crunches against the cold glass. Literally. I explore my scalp and my hair crackles.

The colorkit gel. Right.

I crawl back into the shower, wipe myself up off the floor, and get the water on. Scrub until the mirror fogs and I'm 90 percent sure I'm clean.

I gather my clothes and hurry into the bedroom, opening the closet door with its full-length mirror. Yonni's stark white head bobs in the glass.

I scream, clothes flying, towel crashing to the floor.

"Kit?" Dad, muffled and faint through the bedroom door. "What are you doing in there?"

My face stares from under Yonni's hair. She always had long hair, even at the end, and dyed it white until the grays took over. A pure, soft powder, like light caught and distilled.

My hair is almost translucent, at odds with my black eyebrows and overwide cheeks. I don't look like Mom anymore.

I look like hell.

"Kit," whines Dad from the door, close enough to be right outside it. "You up? I thought we could do breakfast."

I thought you could make me breakfast, he means.

I used to do that, cook for him, when Mom wasn't home. He'd hand me down the pans and plates I was too little to reach, then I'd half burn something semieatable, and we'd watch old feedshows together.

"In a minute," I call. Add a second, softer, "In a minute."

My "new soul" drips water over my shoulders in ghost-white glee, the opposite of Millie.

"Well, Mom, I said you wouldn't exist."

Look at me, keeping my word. And I'm still breathing, so that's Niles covered, too. I show up at work tomorrow, maybe the universe will give me a medal.

I grab a handful of what Yonni used to call my "crowning glory" and stretch it out.

So not worth it.

I throw on some clothes and wrap my new disaster into a tight bun. Grab an old gray hat of Yonni's, with the thin plaid brim, and stuff it on. A few flyaways escape, but for the most part it hides the evidence. I don't look reborn, but at least I'm not a ghost.

I close the closet door and go face Dad.

"There's my baby." He's on the couch, of course, but on the floor by his feet lies a much scuffed digibook—its cover open to reveal a text-filled screen.

A limited edition manufacture of Gilken's collected works, engraved on the back with the old Archive's original seal, annotated by the best scholars of the day.

The digibook that never leaves my bedside table.

I snatch it up. "You went into my room?"

Dad shrugs. "You were gone all day and I never read much of him, and I thought we could—you know—" He smiles as if we're bonding. "He's a pretty interesting guy. Didn't turn out to be such a bad gift, after all."

Right. Because when Mom gave it to me for my seventh birthday, they didn't have the fight from hell over it or any-thing. He didn't spend three hours screaming about how she wasted money we didn't have on a stupid digibook when I could barely even read. Had she even looked at my school reports? And Mom didn't scream back that she got me the book for exactly that reason—because Gilken had trouble with his letters, too, before he became our House's most renowned Scholar. And, of course, I didn't hide under my bed for hours, until snotty tears crusted my skin, because I thought I was getting a puppy.

I hated that book with every fiber of my being. Then Mom left, and I read and reread it until I half had it memorized. Can still quote whole passages verbatim. I fully intended to quote those passages to her. She'd come back because she forgot something, and I'd be ready with my quotes and she'd be so impressed that this time she'd take me with her.

Except she didn't come back.

Then, later, I found her.

"Not okay, Dad." I flatten my palm over the digibook's smooth screen, rub out the smudges. "Not okay."

"I was careful, I promise." He grins, hand to his chest. "Heart swear."

I pause. Dad only heart swears when he's happy, and he's only happy when he's had a drink.

I softly lay the digibook down and lift the juice glass from the couch side table. It smells stringent, earthy, acidic. "*Dad.*"

"What?"

I cross to the kitchen and pour his latest down the sink.

He rises with that fluid grace that means he's had at least one, but not three.

"Wait—lord, Kit, don't you know how much that stuff costs?"

I slam the glass down and grip the sink's edge. Breathe past the hole in my gut. "Get a shower. You're leaving."

"Kit—"

"No, Dad. Just you being here could get me kicked out. It was only supposed to be one night and you've had two."

Not to mention Dee knows he's here.

"Kit—" Whiny and forlorn.

"You know what," I say, "forget the shower. Just go."

He steps forward, smile gone. "Kit, please—"

"Out." I point at the door.

He sags, body and soul. Like I've slit his tendons and he's forgotten to fall. His eyes glaze bright, shine and swim.

It's the alcohol; it's just the alcohol. He is not going to cry.

"I've nowhere to go," he says.

"You'll find something." Or, more likely, someone.

"No, Kit, you don't get it." He sinks to the floor, right there in the middle of the carpet, head in his hands. "He took everything. You see? He took it all. My money, even my *clothes*, and he still says it's not enough." He flings his arms out and almost topples over. "You see this? This is everything I have in the universe, right here. This is it. This, and you."

A chill threads claws down my spine. "What are you talking about? He? He who?"

Dad's hands fall to his lap, eyes drawn over pallid cheeks. "I've nowhere to go and no money to get there."

"Dad, *who*?"

He sinks into himself. "Decker."

"Wait, East 5th Decker?"

The lord of the pawn dealers. Money, drugs, antiques—if it's illegal, Decker's got a hand in it. He can get anyone anything they want, assuming they don't mind offering their soul in exchange. Decker always collects.

I'd gone to him for help with Yonni's pills when Greg and Dee fell through. He'd laughed and said I was a pretty little thing, but those were worth more than I could pay.

Dad collapses into the carpet and cries silent, fat tears. It hurts to look at him. It hurts not to. Everything hurts.

"Don't kick me out, Kit," he says, very soft. "Please."

Begging. He's actually begging.

If he's in trouble with Decker, he'd have to.

"No, shit, Dad, get up. Just get up." I lock my hands behind my neck to run them over my head, except my hat's there. I almost knock it off.

He can't stay. He won't keep quiet, especially if Dee shows again.

Dad gulps air and pulls himself upright, stumbling as if he's had five glasses instead of two.

"How much do you owe?" I ask.

"Fifteen hundred reds," he whispers.

Three months' salary.

Hell.

"Kit—"

"No." I hold both my hands up as if I could push back the words, this truth, his voice. "Shut up and let me think."

Three months' salary. Even if Mr. Remmings hires me back—if—there's energy to cover and food, so it's more like six months. Decker won't wait six months. And the thing about Decker? He'll make you pay up, one way or another. Often in blood.

That's why Greg stole Missa's pain meds. He owed Decker, too.

That's why, when I tracked Greg down to retrieve them, I let him keep half. So that when I next saw my cousin, he wasn't missing a limb or a spleen.

Yonni would have skinned me. She never knew. By the time I returned with the pain meds I had, Missa was dead.

But Greg still has all his internal organs, and so far, so does Dad.

Yonni's gone, and Mom. There's not many of us left.

I close my eyes. "If I cleared the debt, could you manage a room somewhere? Like a boarding tower or something?"

Not stellar living, but clean and cheap.

I've flipped the light switch of Dad, he brightens to near blinding. "You'd do that? Square me with Decker?"

Apparently, I am really this stupid.

"You have to be quiet." I come round the counter and get right in his face. "Don't open the door, don't answer the intercom, don't do *anything*. I'm going to tell everyone you left last night and weren't here the night before. Do *not* make me a liar."

"Oh, Kit, you've no idea—"

"I mean it, Dad. You are *not* here."

He wraps me up, big hands balling in my shirt, breath more juice than alcohol. "I know, baby. I know."

I KNOCK ON MRS. DIVS'S DOOR AND SOMEONE ELSE answers.

"Kit!" A dark-haired blur leaps from the doorway to hug me tight. I stiffen, one arm braced on the colorkit box. She smells like open fields and sunbells, hair swept in a long braid down her bright purple shirt. She pats my shoulder like she's got twenty years on me instead of eight, tops.

Who the hell—?

"You poor thing," she coos, finally backing up for breathing room. "How's your father?"

Oh, right. From yesterday's intercom extravaganza. She's the one who stood up for Dad.

"Uh, fine?" I say.

Mrs. Divs's cane thuds, followed by a cranky, "About time you showed up, I've been waiting all morning."

It's barely even ten.

Her paisley dress swishes her ankles, a green/pink/yellow number that Yonni would have loved. Apparently, paisley was the in thing back when people had no taste.

"Sorry, Mrs. Divs." I glance at the hugger, then ask, "Can I talk to you a minute?"

Her eyebrows rise, but she flaps at the other woman with shaking hands. "Go on then, Annie. I'll see you at the salon later, yeah?"

"Of course!" The hugger beams enthusiasm, big eyes and pearly teeth. "We'll get you fixed right up, Mrs. D, don't you worry." She skips out the door in a bounce of heels and tight pants.

Her perfume sticks to my tongue. "Who's that?"

Mrs. Divs smacks her cane to my shin. I yip.

"*That* is Annie Sheldane, who's only lived here four years and does the best hair in town. And you of all people have no right to be talkin' her down."

"I didn't say anything!"

"Yes, but you thought it." She scans me over, then centers her cane between her spread feet, folding her hands atop it like a general. "And I'm guessing if you'd asked for her help last night, you wouldn't be in that god-awful hat now. Come on, let's see the damage."

Always sharp, Mrs. Divs.

I rub my stinging leg. "I'll pay for the colorkits."

"I don't want to see your money, I want to see your hair."

"There's nothing to see."

"Now that's a lie and you know it."

I hold up the box. "Where should I put this?"

"Anywhere, the table is fine."

I slip past her into her suite and dump the box as directed, while Mrs. Divs fills the doorway, blocking my exit.

"I need a favor," I say.

She sniffs. "I'm listening."

"If someone from the Records Office stops by, can you say that Dad wasn't here? That he left after Dee?"

Her face grows very grave indeed. "You want me to lie for you, Kit?"

There's no making this pretty. "If the Office knows, then Dee can get me kicked out. It's part of Yonni's will. But if all they have is Dee's story . . . no one will believe her over you."

Mrs. Divs taps her pointy-toed foot. "And this is how you steel your fists? By getting your elders to tell stories?"

Partly. The least threatening part. All the parts are a mess.

I stand straight, radiate neutrality, calm. So much calm. "I just need to keep my place."

She sizes me up, chin lifted, eyes narrowed. The one with the power and well aware.

"All right," she says. "I won't mention your father."

The wires in my chest retract their barbs. "Okay. You'll pass the word on to Annie?"

"My, your net keeps getting bigger and bigger. How about I just make sure she's not around at the time?"

Even better. "Thank you, Mrs. Divs. I mean it. You need something, just say."

She points her cane. "Hat."

Well, fair's fair. I flip the brim and reveal all my blinding glory.

Her tiny frame sags. "Oh, Kit."

I had no doubts it was bad. But still—

It's bad.

I slam the hat back on my head. "You're right, I should have asked someone. Too late now."

She thumps closer and pats my scalp. "What did you do?"

"Left it on too long." I edge around her into the hallway.

"How long exactly?"

"Overnight."

"Kit!"

I pause at door. "Yeah?"

Her pink lips weave for a full three seconds, but at last she shakes her head. "You better talk to that boy, if you're making the rounds. He's up in 308."

Niles.

I don't know that I want to talk to Niles.

My hand tightens on the doorframe. "Has . . . he been here long? When did he move in?"

Mrs. Divs's mouth takes on a sly little twitch. I shouldn't have asked. "He hasn't," she says, "not as such. You remember old Mr. Green, don't you? That's his grandson. He's here for a seasonal internship or some such. Mr. Green moved to North 9th you know, after that last surgery. Deathly afraid of elevators and couldn't do the stairs. Such a sweet man. His grandson seems sweet, too, so don't you go snapping at him."

Too late for that.

"Thanks," I say, again, and close the door.

I WAKE NILES UP. HIS HAIR FLIES EVERY WHICH WAY, dark pants slung low, ribbed shirt only half tucked in. It's a Greg outfit. That Niles somehow makes it look sexy says something—and nothing good.

Though even at Greg's spiffiest, he wouldn't know sexy if it knocked him in the jaw. He tried to come on to me once, when he was way too blissed out to know better or even who I was. He didn't remember when he sobered up. Wish I could likewise.

My nose scrunches, and I shake the memory away.

Niles straightens, tucks in his shirt, smooths his flyaway hairs, and suddenly he's so far from Greg they might not exist in the same House—Greg a bug and Niles a lordling.

I stare. Or gape. Take your pick.

"I see you kept your promise," he says.

"I tend to do that," I say.

"Okay, let's try another." He holds out his hand. "Not today, or tonight, either."

I close my eyes. Why did I come up here?

Why, why, why?

"This isn't why I came," I say.

"Then we'll cover this, first."

I blink my eyes open and he still stands, lordling-style, hand out. I stare from it to him, but he doesn't back down and his fingers don't drop.

"How about an exchange?" I ask.

He eases back a bit, head tilting. "Oh?"

"Can you forget Dad was here last night? No matter who asks?"

His expression rivals Mrs. Divs's. "Like the Enactors?"

Yep. He's a quick one.

"Yes." Probably a good idea. I'm sure they all talk to each other. "But more like the Records Office. Any housing officials."

His stare drills, and I'd offer a lung to be counting dust mites instead of staring back—especially as his face blanks out into nothing. But looking away means giving up.

"Do I get to know why?" he asks.

"Yonni's will—she's my grandmother. Was my—whatever, the will says I can't have family stay overnight. If I do, then the suite's forfeit and the Records Office can claim it."

His blankness slides into confusion. "Why?"

"She hated her kids? And she thought . . ."

You always let those idiots tie you in knots, Yonni said, when her skin had turned to paste and her eyes to holes, and we both knew the new meds weren't going to cut it. *Now, I know you promised you'll do better, but I also know what a little liar you are, so this will make sure.* She tapped the digisheet of the will she just signed.

I'm not a liar, I'd said. A lie in itself.

"Thought what?" Niles asks.

I shake my head. "That I'd do exactly what I'm doing. You in or what?"

He considers me and then the paneling across the hall, as if working all the angles. Though at a guess, I'd bet money he'd made his choice the minute it was offered. Just a feeling.

"Not today and not tonight," he says.

"Okay," I say.

"Okay."

That was . . . easy. I slide back a step. "Thanks."

His hands slide in his pockets and he rocks on his toes. "So . . . you hungry?" He doesn't wink. He might as well.

"No," I say.

"We could get breakfast."

"I'm booked."

"Really?" He leans in, voice dropping low. "Not with those idiots at the market. Because it seems to me the last time you met up with them, that one girl pulled a knife."

He's too close and familiar by half, and with apparently zero respect for my brain.

"Why absolutely," I say. "We plan to dance naked on tables and recite the Archivist's Oath backward."

"In that case." He slips into his suite, grabs what looks like a wallet from a side table, and rejoins me in the hall.

"Let's roll."

"You're not serious."

"Why not?" He saunters past me toward the stairs. "I love getting naked on tables."

Yeah, and if he's not careful, I'll stake him to one.

"Do you want to get decked?"

"Did I come knocking on your door? No?" He swings into the stairwell, and bows me inside. "After you."

Well, hell.

"SO, WHERE ARE WE GOING?" NILES JOGS BACKWARD in front of me, unafraid of the cracked sidewalks or potential pedestrians.

"*We* are going nowhere." I speed-walk past him. He turns midstride and matches pace. It's not even noon yet and the walkway fizzes under our feet. My shoes want to melt. So does my scalp, damp and icky under the hat. It gets any hotter and the universe will just have to deal with my hair.

Niles nods at my hat. "Disaster?"

"How did you know?" I ask.

"Last night, you go home with a box of colorkits. This morning? Hat." He salutes. "All hail my devastating powers of deduction."

I roll my eyes.

He flicks the hat's brim. "It's cute, I like it."

A streethover zooms by and I slip into the scattered traffic, crest the whoosh of speed and horns, and hit the other side.

Niles pulls out a traffic dance of his own and slides next to my elbow. "I thought we agreed, not today."

"I wasn't—you going to bring that up every five seconds?"

"Kind of hard to forget." He shrugs, arms held close like he doesn't know what to do with them.

Last night, he had them wrapped around me.

Yeah, so I wouldn't go splat on the floor.

I stop and turn. Ahead, the street branches in a Y. Left for Low South, right for East 5th. For all Niles can swing the Greg vibe, he doesn't seem the seedy type. Especially out here, with the sun catching his flyaways and gleaming off his skin.

I probably gleam, too. The air's sticky enough.

"It's safe," I say. "I kept my word last night, right? You don't have to guard your investment. Go home."

He shifts back on his heels. "You really don't like me."

"It's not about liking. I've stuff to do, and you don't want to be involved. Trust me." I flick a thumb over my shoulder, toward East 5th. "Go home."

I swing down the right branch of the Y. Niles doesn't take the hint. Three steps and he's beside me again.

"Go home," I say.

Another shrug. "Where do you think I grew up?"

"Wait, East 5th? But . . ." I glance over, reevaluate. He looks so clean. No obvious scars, at least not in profile. Even his nose is straight. "It didn't break you?"

His mouth twists on something that should be a smile, and isn't. "You don't know that, either."

I guess not. Yonni and I were in East 5th for a while before Missa gave us the suite, and it's not like I have scars.

That's why she gave us the suite, and why Yonni accepted. We had a few close calls, or rather I had a few close calls. One bad one in an alley that Greg got me out of. Another reason I let him keep half Missa's meds.

"You're right," I say. "I don't."

We walk in silence. Low South fights for dominance for a few blocks, upkeep battling age, but eventually the grime wins out. Skytowers loom in old heavy skestone, chipped and faded. People hunch into themselves, or dare the world to give a damn. The world never takes the bet.

We're quiet as the towers slink together. The half-constructed skeleton of a high-class hotel, a listing line of residences with busted screens, a small grocery with dead things in the window.

I hang a left down the alley with the teeth graffiti—a long row of white molars painted with the stuff that burns green in direct sunlight. Not that this place has ever seen sunlight. We pass between rusty escape lifts and metal doors with busted access panels. Niles shifts closer to me, elbow brushing my arm.

Near the end of the alley, just around the corner from the other street lies another identically gritty door with a busted panel.

Decker has very specific hours. He's closed tomorrow but should be open today.

I bang the door with the side of my fist. Niles does his blank-out thing, elbow frozen near mine. He's an East 5th'er all right. He knows where we are.

I meet his eyes. "Really. Go home."

The tension disappears at speed and he grins. "What are you talking about? I like an adventure."

Maybe I misread the tension thing.

The door cracks and Decker sticks his skinny neck out. "What the hell do you—well, my, my, my. If it isn't the asshole's kid sister. I thought you were too good for us."

"Cousin," I say. "And have you seen the feeds? I'm not good enough for shit. Can I come in?"

Niles's eyes narrow, but he's not the important one here.

Decker widens the door and leans into the space, head outstretched as if to sniff me. He's got big eyes and bony arms and bright clothes that scream for attention. "Maybe. Who's he?"

No one Decker needs to have on his radar.

"Just some guy from the district," I say. "Didn't want me walking the 5th alone."

"Which district?"

"Mine. Can we come in?"

"No." Decker flashes teeth as wide and long as the graffiti's. "Not we, you. Come on." He waggles his fingers and steps inside.

Good. Niles doesn't need to be in the middle of this.

I shoot him a nod and follow Decker.

Niles takes my arm with light fingers, voice dropping low, "What are you doing?"

"What? I have to." I shake him off and step through the door. It slams shut.

A narrow hall stretches into darkness, with a spitting overhead light. The walls peel. The floor creaks.

"Well, well, well," says Decker, sliding past me to creak his way forward. "And what's the elusive daughter of the infamous Millie have to say for herself?"

"Elusive?" I ask.

Decker winks at me over his shoulder. "Nice hat."

Like it'd stop anyone from recognizing me. Didn't stop him.

Decker's shadow chases the dark and mine gets tangled in his steps. We reach the end of the hall, and he pushes the final door open onto a universe of junk. Piles, tables, and shelves of old mugs, dataslates, pillows, figurines, furniture, dishware, circuits, and who knows what all. Decker shimmies his way through the mess to the big glass counter in the center of the room, yellow in the yellow light. He swings around behind it, spreads his palms on its smudged top.

The last time I was here, Yonni's pendant lay on that counter—its green vines entwined protectively over a lonely red heart. Missa had given it to Yonni for their anniversary. Greg had swiped it from her dresser. I grabbed the pendant before the sale could go through and hauled Greg's thieving ass out.

Decker leans forward, as if the memory plays in his head, too. "And to what do I owe this unexpected pleasure?"

"Dad," I say. "I'm here to clear his debt."

Whole data systems run at speed behind Decker's eyes. "Mmm Ricky? Yes, Ricky Franks."

I reach into my pocket and lay Yonni's heart on the counter. It beats softly from the mesh circuits inside, isolated. Betrayed.

"This cover it?" I ask, flat.

Decker's eyes narrow and he sniffs. "Isn't this the piece you'd see your brother's ass in hell over?"

"Cousin, and this covers it."

Decker reaches for the heart with spider fingers, and I have to curl my own to keep from snapping his off.

"A Pulsebeat Echo 38–9." He lifts it in his palm, strokes its subtle beats. "Pretty. But it was pretty the first time round."

Yes. Back when I had a soul I wouldn't sell.

"Is. The debt. Covered?"

Decker sighs and rocks. "I don't know, will I actually get to keep it this time?"

"Decker." Full of warning. He may be the lord of East 5th, but that's Yonni's soul between his pawing fingers.

"You're the one who came to me, girl." He catches my eye and sighs again. "All right, all right. I'd say this is worth six hundred reds?"

"A thousand, and you know it." Which is a hundred more than he quoted Greg and likely less than half what it's worth.

And still five hundred short of Dad's debt.

Decker barks, laugh pitched deep for his high voice.

"You're in dreamland, dearie."

I hold out my palm. "Then hand it back."

His fingers close automatically, eyes taking on the same lust they'd had the last time around. I've already pried it from his clasp once, with him cursing up hell while Greg freaked out. I'll do it again.

"A thousand or nothing," I say.

There are other dealers in the city. I don't know who they are or where they are, but I'll find them, get a better price, and come back with actual reds.

"You're as crazy as your mother."

Doesn't matter what hand you're dealt, Yonni aways said. *You play the cards you have.*

I reach over the counter and grab his wrist to drive that point home. "Yep."

He's got thick bones despite his lack of muscle. If he calls my bluff, I'm screwed.

If he calls my bluff, I can just reach for the naked steel woman holding up a serving plate on the end of the counter and hit him over the head with it.

Decker tries to pull away. I hold fast.

"You think you're some Enactor Shadow or something? Get your hands off me!"

"Give me the pendant."

"Why did I let her in?" he asks the ceiling, pathetic and abused. "Why, why?"

"The pendant."

His gaze flips to me. "You do like to repeat yourself, don't you?"

I squeeze tighter. My hand aches. My arm too. He better do something soon, because there's no way I can keep this up.

He grins. Actually grins. "Oh, I do like my pretties with bite. All right. A thousand. But if I remember right, for daddy dearest, that still leaves you five hundred short. Maybe we could come to an arrangement?"

Not that kind, we can't.

I let go and manage not to shake out my aching fingers. "I've got another piece for you."

His ears perk up. Literally.

"Another Pulsebeat? My girl, what crypts have you raided?"

"No." I pull my last bit of pawn-ability from my pocket and toss it on the counter. "A bracelet."

It shimmers, and its silver threads and dangle charms seem to float. A coiled, sparkling snake.

It'd spun snakelike from Mom's wrist, too, whenever she moved her arm. Sleek and subtle, like the neat knot of her hair and the silky weave of her clothes. Each charm represented a place—planets, cities, waterfalls—all far away and some even out of House. Beyond Galton's borders, and into the Houses of Westlet or Fane. I know, because watching it was easier than watching her.

The last night I saw her, she'd slipped it off her wrist and laid it in my palm.

"Ooo." Decker lays the pendant down, forgotten, to claim his next prize. He holds it up to the light so the charms flutter yellow. Far away wonders from distant planets.

You've the whole world, remember?

The whole world.

Decker purses his lips and tilts his head in a whole "It's pretty, but mostly worthless" routine, then glances at me.

I don't know what my face is doing, but it wipes the smile off his.

"Four hundred," he says.

Holy hell. I thought he'd come back with half that. Mom can't have put much money in it. But then, she did like to throw money around.

"Eight," I say. That'd give me three hundred over what Dad owes, enough to set him up somewhere else.

He laughs, a breathy, soundless thing. "You're joking."

Probably, but I don't much care.

"You're the expert. You tell me."

He tries to pry me apart, second by glaring second. I cross my arms and let him work. If he's looking for a soul, I haven't one to speak of.

Or won't, after this.

"You know," he sets down the bracelet and leans in to sniff. "I could use someone like you. Want a job?"

I blink slow, drag out my syllables. "Bracelet."

He waves his finger at my nose. "A bit repetitive, but honestly doesn't give a shit. I could use you."

I slap my hand over the bracelet on the counter, and Decker's oily fingers cover mine. "Don't be hasty, now. I'm just sayin'."

He reaches into his pocket with his free hand, pulls out a transaction card, and holds it to his mouth.

"Load three hundred reds," he says. The card's thin flexi-digit coating flashes 3 0 0. I pull my own card out, scratched and bent at one edge, and tell it to "Find transactent."

It blinks blue and beeps at the found signal.

"Send," says Decker.

My card fills with numbers that calculate at speed, ending in 3 0 0. A counterpoint to his card's three zeros.

Odd, my card still feels like the empty one. Or maybe that's my chest, its center lost between Decker's grubby fingers.

That's it, then. The worst of it was done.

Decker purrs. "Excellent. I'd about given up hope of getting any money out of Ricky."

"He's clear?" I ask.

"He's clear, and lucky in his choice of offspring, I must say."

I pocket my transaction card and do *not* look at Yonni's heart.

"Always a pleasure," says Decker. "Next time we meet, try not to manhandle me."

There won't be a next time. My only other thing of value is the suite. If Dad screws himself over, he'll just be screwed. I turn for the hall. "Thanks, Decker."

"I'm serious about the job, you know. Come back anytime."

The alley blinds me after the corridor's dark, teeth gaping in a crooked smirk. I make a beeline for the street. Out of the underbelly and into the mouth.

"Hey!" Niles's voice, then the boy himself jogs at my elbow. I don't slow. We break into the street and I bound across the thoroughfare.

He keeps up. "I take it that didn't go well."

It went great. It went perfectly. Dad's clear, Decker's happy, and everything's gone exactly to plan.

I'm going to be sick.

"Are you ever going home?" I ask.

I might not have spoken. He skips it entirely. "Decker's bad news, you shouldn't—"

"*What?*" I skid to a stop and round on him. "What is up with you? What do you want?"

"Not to end up on the wrong side of Decker. He murders people, or didn't you know?"

"How would *you* end up on Decker's wrong side?"

He leans close. "I hate to bust your bubble, but death-via-Decker breaks our contract. You want me to keep my mouth shut? Stay away from him."

"God *dammit.*" I run my hands over my head, catching my hat as it slips off.

This *day.* Dad, this idiot, Decker—God, Decker—and Yonni's beating heart in his grasping, oily hands.

And there's no way in hell I can jump off ledges now, even without that stupid promise—Yonni's ghost would find me and skin me and kick me out.

"Whoa," says Niles.

I look around for the next neon disaster, but he's staring at my head.

Right. The disaster that already happened.

I throw the hat against the streetside tower wall. It bounces to the cracked pavement.

"Can't you just go home?" I ask.

His gaze never leaves my hair. "Okay, let's go."

"You, not me."

His eyebrows arc, the *not likely* practically audible.

I move to the nearest streetlight and lean into the hot metal. Stare up into the skytowers with sharp, jagged roofs.

"This could all have been so over by now," I say, quiet. Days over. All I had to be was faster. All I had to do was jump.

"Hey." Niles steps closer, humor gone. "Am I really bothering you?"

"Seriously?" I ask and the exhaustion creeps in.

"Right." For some reason, that hits home. His hands dig deep into his pockets, and for one stupid second I want to reach out and tell him it's fine, everything's okay.

Not a damn thing in the universe is okay.

I thump my head against the pole. "Look, it's not *you* you, but I have to sort out family and you're making it hard."

"Was that what Decker was about?" Niles asks.

"That's what everything is about."

He takes in the cracked streetlight casings, the barred tower windows, me. "You know, I get it. The mom thing. My old man left me with a reputation, too, and some things you can't live down. Sometimes you can't see things worth living for." His voice drops and there's something nice about it, in whispers. A quiet register that reverberates.

"Yeah, well." I kick at the cracks in the walkway. "This isn't about Mom."

I sold her off with Yonni's heart.

We're silent amid the lurking traffic. The sun tries to bake us on the pavement.

He checks his watch. "Breakfast is shot, so . . . lunch?"

I shake my head. "I'm not done yet."

"You're going back to—?"

"No, just stupid stuff. The rest is easy." Or should be, with luck. With the debt paid, it's just finding Dad a room.

"Want company?" he asks.

"I'll still be here tomorrow, you have my word."

"That's not why I was asking." He smiles. Half smiles. The way uncertainty catches its edges, it might not be a smile at all.

Oh.

"Go home," I say.

"Okay." He slides back a couple steps, and suddenly there is space. Breathing room. I like breathing room. It breathes.

He turns to go.

"I'd be up for dinner," I say.

He pauses, hair brushing his neck as his head turns. He winks. "Done."

I am such an idiot.

"IT'S A DAY-TO-DAY THING," SAYS THE GUY BEHIND THE desk. "We don't do long terms."

The boarding tower clerk is the inverse of Decker— short, small-eyed, and muscled. He owns the counter while barely able to see over it. I don't impress him. The looming giant at my elbow vying for attention doesn't impress him, either. In fact, the clerk looks about two seconds from bouncing the giant out the door. "No," he says.

"But Gerry," says the giant. "I need another night!"

"Get me the reds, Lend."

"But Gerry—"

"Reds or nothing. Out." The clerk jerks a thumb over his shoulder, toward the small back entrance that might as well be a revolving door. It rattles and competes with the chatter. The ornate front doors are glass-less, boarded and barred, their carved starscapes half-hidden by scrap.

The giant storms off, and I slide into his spot. "I have reds."

"I only accept funds from them as is paying," says the clerk. "And we don't do long terms. What you doing here, anyway? This is a male establishment."

"It's for my dad and he's not responsible, so—"

"Don't I know you from somewhere?" The clerk squints at me, supremely uninterested in anything coming out of my mouth.

"No," I say.

"You look familiar." He leans in a little, ignoring my hair for my face.

I brace for the inevitable.

A skeleton with skin pops up beside the counter and hip-butts me out of the way. The clerk sighs. "What you want, Jo?"

I slip away from the desk and toward a pillar before the clerk figures out how he knows me. The lobby has several pillars, soaring up to third-story heights. This tower was something once—an old sky-rated hotel maybe, or a lordling residential. The walls are wood and inlaid with glass. The stone floor is seamless below the pockmarks. There's even a grand staircase flanked by golden pillars. Give the sixteen or so guys spread-eagled on its steps some laundered clothes and data-feed ear clips, and this place could double for the House Lord's skytower.

Assuming it was scrubbed by an army.

Not a bad place as such. Dad will do okay here. Greg did okay here. It's where he came the first time he sobered up. Or the second. This will work.

As long as I swing by and pay for Dad's bed every morning.

If I hand Dad my transaction card, the first place he'll hit is the bar.

The room goes dark. Pitch black. The lights, the fuzzy

wall-screen in the corner, the whirring fans overhead—all throttled.

I freeze. Of all the places to be stuck in a power-out. Didn't we just have one of these?

The whole room groans.

"God dammit! I didn't pay no fifty reds to live in some damn cave!" yells a deep bass voice, followed by the clerk's resigned, "Sammy, check the breakers."

The pillar was straight ahead of me. I step forward, arm out, until my fingers hit warm stone. I slide around the side.

"It's the third time this week!" Deep Voice continues.

"Second," says the clerk. "And I can't help when the grid shuts down."

"Don't you 'second' me, Gerry! I know what I—"

The lights blink on. Power-outs never last long, five minutes tops.

"About time," says Deep Voice, who turns out to be a shirtless guy propped against the pillar behind mine. He has more meat than the skeleton, but not enough for a voice like that—especially when compared to the guy with the broad chest and ghost skin, who furtively glances around the same pillar like he's looking for someone.

Our eyes lock.

The power technician from the museum's rooftop.

I walk forward. "Hey, what are you—" but I swallow

the *doing here*. It's a boarding tower, and one of the better ones in the district. Power technicians must make less than I thought. "Uh . . . hey."

The verbal save that wasn't.

"You?" he asks. "What are you doing here?"

He's dressed better than I've seen him—the whole two times—in slacks and a dark button-up. Quality stuff, from the way it falls as he shifts his weight. What a fidget looks like on a two-hundred-pound man.

"Trying to rent a room," I say.

"Ha ha!" barks the guy on the floor. "Ain't no room for you here, girlie."

"So I'm told."

The power tech hustles me toward an empty stretch of wall, away from the cranky complaints lobbied from the staircase and the static voices from the wall-screen's newscast. He jerks his head at Deep Voice. "He's not wrong. This ain't no place for you."

"It's for my dad."

"You'd land your dad here?"

"He can't stay with me."

The power tech doesn't answer. His face expounds for him.

I'm a god-awful daughter. Suitable spawn for a god-awful mom.

"Look," I start, and the lights go out. Again.

"You've got to be kidding me," I say, and the room agrees—loud and pissed. One power-out isn't that unusual, but two in succession? That's not a city power-grid glitch, that's a faulty tower circuit. Harsh voices clamor between "I want a damn refund!" and "This is unacceptable, you hear me, Gerry?"

The power tech doesn't join in.

"You looked into the circuits here?" I ask. "It's your job, right?"

"I don't work for free," says the techie.

The wall-screen flickers on in the opposite corner. Nothing else, not the lights or the fans, just the lone screen in the dark.

"Attention," says a sleek female voice, light and razor-edged. "If I could borrow your attention for a sec."

Mom.

My heart falls out of my mouth and I can't feel my hands. *Mom.*

The screen crackles and there she is. Smiling with her too-wide mouth, dark hair swept high. Her airy purple blouse has the Archivist symbol stitched into the collar. The same hairstyle and blouse she wore the night she died.

The night she blew up the House Archive.

"That's better," she says. "Now, I assume you all know

who I am? Excellent. Then you know you cannot stop me. I hope you've enjoyed your ravaged energy, but this is the end. You will be held to Account."

The feed fizzes, separates into static, stringy color that realigns into an ad for upmarket shoes. Sleek men's shoes with low heels. The same ad that pops up between everyday feedshows. Regular programming.

The lights return. Blare. Colors and movement and a host of raised voices, none of them Mom's.

She's dead.

She was right here.

She's *dead*.

"Hey." A hand touches my arm, and I jump from my skin.

I swing round. "*What?*"

The power tech, eyes pissed and mouth determined. "Wasn't that your mother? What the hell?"

I shake him off. "I can't talk about this."

I can't think about this. I can't even breathe.

My chest cycles windstorms. All I do is breathe.

She's dead.

That was her voice. I'd forgotten.

No, I hadn't. She talked in my dream. And even if she didn't, she's a hack-bomber who kills people, so what do I care?

The techie clasps my arm. "What do you mean you can't

talk about it? She's on the damn feeds, girl! That ain't a luxury you get."

"What do you want me to say? She's *dead*."

The room roars, fear and anger. The righteous indignation of the wronged. They do know her, have been hurt as the whole city has been hurt. Punished for the bloodlings' past sins.

Mom held the rear access door of the Archive open for me that night. Snuck me past security. "I'm so glad you came!" she'd said, like a little kid. Like we were getting away with something. "I was afraid I wouldn't get to show you where I worked."

My museum tour had run late, and I didn't think I'd make her highly specific time frame. Something to do with guard rotations. "I could have just come tomorrow," I said.

She smiled. She had a pretty smile. "No, you really couldn't."

"What did she mean?" asks the techie, shaking me a little. "What was she on about? What 'end'?"

I twist out of his grasp. "I don't know, okay?"

And I don't, except that Mom's vengeance always meant paying back in kind.

"Hey, you!" says another and all too familiar voice. "Back off her!"

Greg. Lean, lanky, pretty in an oily way. His shirt was

nice once, a paisley button-up that was probably somebody else's. The sleeves are too long. So are his curls. They flop into his eyes, oily and frizzy at once. He sidles up next to us, strutting manfully while also taking care to keep me between him and power tech's beefy frame.

"What are you doing here?" I ask.

"What do you think?" His glare balances between lethal and sullen. "Some of us don't have anywhere else to live."

I clutch my head. Of course. Of *course*. If it isn't Mom's fault, it's mine. And it's not like this isn't the place I helped Greg get a room in before, way back when we were still speaking. What did I expect?

"The real question is, what are you doing here?" Greg flicks my hair off my ear, shaky knuckles brushing my temple. "This looks like hell, by the way."

"So do you."

He grins. The same grin he gave me when we were kids, missing tooth and all. His hand drops to my shoulder and rubs. "Aw, rough day?"

"This your boyfriend?" The power tech's disapproval is almost tactile.

"I said back off, man." Greg takes my elbow and hauls me aside. "Kit, I need to talk to you."

"I already had it out with Dee, talk to her." There's nothing to say, and enough people are talking already—like the whole male mob yelling about Mom. The air practically pulses anger, and at some point the clerk's going to piece together why I look familiar.

I shake Greg off and head to the rear door, skirting the crowd and keeping to the shadows. I make the alley without mishap, slamming into heat thick enough to eat my lungs.

"Kit, wait up!" Greg's only three steps behind. He grabs hold of my shirt. "I told you, we need to talk."

Damn guys and their grabby hands.

I twist free. "Keep your voice down! You want to get me killed?"

The power tech follows next, closing the door with a soft groan. His bulky mass fills the alley even more than the dumpster at my elbow. "I thought that's what you were goin' for."

Greg jumps. "What the hell?"

"Oh, drop it already," I tell the techie. "You've done your good deed, call it done."

"What good deed?" asks Greg.

The power tech glares murder.

Greg throws up his hands, sleeves sagging down his bony arms. "You know what? I don't care." He leans in to whisper-spit in my ear, "I need to talk to you. Alone."

He jerks his chin at the techie, who unfolds his arms and prowls forward. They crowd the alley between them, skinny and bulky, rumpled and crisp, and both determined for answers.

I need space, fresh air, and quiet. Maybe one of Mrs. Divs's cookies, or even dinner with someone who survived East 5th.

I need Mom's voice out of my head.

"Later, Greg, okay? I—have a date." Or a dinner. Whatever. It works.

Or doesn't. Greg snorts. "Like hell. I'm just asking for five minutes here—"

"Fine, I'll pay your room for a week. After that, you're on your own." With the bracelet money, I should have enough. "I'll be back tonight with Dad."

"Tonight won't cut it," says Greg.

"Well, it'll have to." I spin on my heel and sprint for the street.

"Hey," calls the power tech as Greg swears, but the only pounding steps are mine. Until something heavy thuds. Crashes? I glance back and stop dead.

The techie's on the ground. Face-first, something thin and silver stuck in the back of his neck. He doesn't move. Greg stands over him.

"Shit, I didn't want to do that," says Greg.

He's killed him. Greg killed the power tech.

No. No, oh *hell* no.

"Dammit, Greg." I run back and sink to my knees. The techie isn't bleeding. I twist his face off the pavement, gently. His nose bleeds, cheeks scraped red. I search for a pulse. Where is it? Where *is* it?

"What the hell? What did you do?" I reach for the silver tube in the techie's neck, and a cold circle touches the base of mine. It bites, sharp and deep.

I reach for it but my fingers haven't weight. "G-Greg?"

"Sorry, Kit. Really," he says, as the world powers out.

LIGHTNING SHOOTS THROUGH MY BONES AND SNAPS
me straight. I sit up, nerves pinging like a vid arcade.

"Easy, easy." Hands on my waist, squeezing soft, trying
to keep my scattered guts in place.

Yeah, good luck. They don't fit. My skin looks intact, but
everything underneath fizzes crossways. In about three seconds, I'll explode. I can see it. A sparking mess of white and
blue that doesn't fade when I blink. Or don't blink. Maybe I
haven't. It looks the same either way.

The hand transfers to my back and rubs. "Deep breaths.
It'll fade in a minute. Let it do its thing. Breathe."

The hand takes on rhythm, pushing inhales up my
spine and smoothing down on the release. A calm touch. A
calm voice.

Maybe my heart won't claw its way out of my throat.

I breathe. The sparks lessen, coalesce. Fade.

I'm in a room, I think. A rope light hangs from . . . somewhere, half its woven glow-tubes busted. Darkness swallows the ceiling at its base and blankets the world outside
our narrow cone of chairs and faces.

Dirty fold-up chairs and two faces, caught between
shadow and glow. Besides the man with the calm voice, I
see one woman and one man—a girl and a boy. Ardent, grim,
and watching me.

Bad. Very bad. They have East 5th all over them, which

means whatever they want will probably kill me.

Or not. There's always worse.

I jump to my feet. My chair crashes, my head spins, and the sparks return with a vengeance.

My feet will not keep steady. My brain claws at my skull.

"I told you we shouldn't trust the jitterbug," says the girl. She sounds . . . familiar?

"You're just pissed 'cause it worked," says the calm one, a rumble against my ear as he rubs my shoulder.

Off. He needs to get his damn hands off.

"Worked? Look at her! She can't even process."

"Give her a minute. Clarity is strong shit."

Clarity? They flushed my system with *Clarity*? God, that would revive the dead.

Was I dead?

No, I can't be. I promised.

I push away from Mr. Chest. The room bounces like a puppy. "What the hell did you hit me with?"

The guy reaches for me, and I throw out my arm, palm up and splayed. I stumble, but the floor doesn't get me. "Back up. Just back the hell up."

"Okay, okay. Take it easy." The calm one raises his hands and keeps his distance. "He wasn't supposed to dose you, I swear. We only gave him the stuff in case he couldn't ditch your Shadow."

"Emergency only," mutters the girl. "Which it wasn't."

"You saw her after he dosed the guy," Calm hisses low. "He didn't have a choice."

"Also a mistake," she shoots back. "You think you can just dose one of them and get away with it? We probably have a whole Enactor contingent on our ass."

"*His* ass," Calm amends. "We didn't dose anyone."

"Shut up," I say under my breath. My palms flatten on my throbbing temples so they won't combust. I'm missing something. Darkness curls through my vision and somewhere the universe is breaking, and I can't tell what's real unless they all . . . "*Shut up*," I yell.

They freeze. Caught midsentence in the glowlight.

"Where the hell am I?" I ask.

The calm one opens his mouth, but I hold up my hand. I may only get one question, and there's a better question, more important. I can almost see it. Stained pavement between looming walls. Oily curls and metal-grated doors.

The power tech on the ground. The spike at my neck.

I search my skin and find the hole—small, raised, and sore as hell.

Greg.

Anger settles my bones. The room stops its shimmy and my body doesn't sway. "Where is the power tech?"

They shift, straighten. A readying of hands and feet.

"Power tech?" asks the girl.

The calm one glances between her and me. "The Shadow?"

My fists clench, finger by finger. "I mean the man Greg dosed before me. Is. He. Dead?"

"The Shadow," he reiterates, slower. "No, he's fine. I made Greg drag him into the boarding tower. We don't need that kind of trouble."

"That's why we pulled in the jitterbug to begin with," says the girl. "So your tail wouldn't catch on. Not that *that's* worked."

"You think the power tech's a spy," I say. Not just any spy, but from the Enactors' hidden elite. A boarding tower live-in who fixes museum roofs. If they dumped him unconscious in the tower, his fellow boarders would have robbed him blind. Which means I'll owe him a room, if they're right and Greg didn't—

If Greg—

"Greg sold me out," I say just to hear the truth of it. Feel the weight. My cousin stuck a needle in my neck and probably a bow on my pretty, packaged head. And the worst part? The ultimate, absolute ache?

I didn't guess, wouldn't have thought. Not that he'd attack me. Not this.

Maybe he'd steal the shirt from your back, but not the

skin from your bones.

"I'm going to rip his spine out his throat," I say, matter-of-fact.

The calm one eases a step back even as he holds out a hand. "Hey, easy now, that's not it at all. We just needed to talk to you without the Shadow."

"So you had him dose me?"

His fizzy eyebrows bunch in a single thick line. "I told you, that wasn't our idea."

"I don't care whose—" I stop, blink, and my brain kicks in.

Fizzy eyebrows. A fit, muscled girl who could take the whole room down single-handed. A skinny, silent boy with big, pretty eyes.

The Outer Brink kids from the Low South Market.

I'm stuck in a hole in the dark with people who think my mother a god.

"She remembers," the skinny one singsongs out of nowhere, so bright the light stutters. I jump and even the calm one flinches.

"Dammit, Sans," says the calm one. "Give a man some warning."

"If you remember," says the girl to me, "then you know what we want."

"That'd be a 'no,'" I say.

The girl is out of the chair and in my face. "You may think this funny, but it's *our* home on the line. Where the hell is Millie Oen?"

"Dead," I say into her clear blue eyes.

Her fist rams my stomach. Pain explodes, rocketed together, pressed and screaming and I can't, I can't, I can't—

Scream. Don't scream.

I stumble, hug the hole where my stomach was. Is? Hell.

"What the hell?" The calm one grabs her arm and pulls her back. "Take it easy."

"She's screwing around," says the girl.

"She's barely awake!"

"We don't have *time*." The girl shakes him off and circles the chairs, pointing at me. "Look at her! Look. Has she freaked out? Has she even screamed? You really think she won't screw us regardless?"

As one, they turn and stare. I might be a poisonous, hissing snake. Or the daughter of vengeful god.

Next time, I'm splitting everyone's eardrums three times over.

Metal clangs against metal, harsh, distant echoes from below or above or wherever the hell is close but not *here*.

The light goes out.

The calm one swears up a spark storm, while the skinny kid whispers, "They're here."

Hell, someone else? Decker? Enactors?

Enactors, probably. They have Shadows on the brain.

"How can they be here?" the calm one rounds on the girl. "The building's clean, we haven't used it before. You told me it was clean."

"You gave me five minutes to check," she says.

He jerks a thumb at me. "I was hauling her ass around!"

"And I told you not to give the jitterbug the damn doser!"

"Shut *up*," I say. "It's hard enough to think already."

I blink through the fog in my head and the bite in my gut, for all the good it does. The dark is almost thick enough to touch.

"You take her," says the calm one. "Sans, with me."

Like hell she will.

I spin on my heel and bolt.

Which sends my footfalls echoing all over the damn room.

"Who took off? That you, Tress?" asks Calm, becoming less calm by the second.

A soft curse and the echoes double. The girl's following.

I close my eyes and feel the floor. Hard and slick, then harsh and grated, and back again. Every step feels like the next one won't be there.

Beyond the dark—the space, the room—metal clangs, again, follow by softer thuds. Steps? Sparkguns?

My footsteps multiply by dozens.

They're following. All of them. A pounding pulse my chest reiterates. I veer left or maybe right—just enough so the echoes shift behind me.

At some point, I'll smack something. The room can't go on forever. I stretch my arms in front of me, palms out.

This is going to hurt like hell.

I slam into the wall hands first—bones crunching into each other, ignore, ignore—and push off with the recoil. Their stomps fill the room, the world, my head.

I skid to the side, fingers scraping over metal—sound, too much sound—for a frame, window, door, anything.

A harsh smack. Someone else found the wall. "Ow! Ow ow ow." High, male.

I don't slow, palm picking up splinters and rust flakes.

There has to be a door. Has to. No one builds a room without a door.

My fingers catch and there it is, a frame. I skim the edge toward the low center. Over, left, down, *handle.*

I grab, twist, push through—then swing round behind to slam myself between it and the inside wall. Hold my breath.

Greg showed me this trick, ages ago. He's going to wish he hadn't.

The steps pound past and I count. They merge in an

impossible din, echoes bouncing in all directions. Enough to cover the lack of mine. This room is bigger or has a higher ceiling.

The echoes grow tinny. Replaced by my heart, which wants to explode.

Not yet, you don't. Not yet.

I slowly lean sideways and peek my head around the door. Pitch-black dark.

Whoever else is here may be in there, but at least I know for a fact the Brinkers aren't.

I ease out from behind the door and slip my shoes off to maintain the quiet. Trail my hand over the scraped metal and reenter the room we started in. Continue my previous trajectory along the wall. I run on tiptoe, holding my shoes, ears straining. No new echoes. No sound apart from my breath.

Which would make sense of Enactors, especially Shadows. They're trained to be silent and have all the latest gear. Like night-vision sensors. They could be tracking me from across the room. They could be sneaking up behind me now. I can just feel it, their breath on my neck—

I bite my tongue and run faster.

My hand hits a corner and I slide round. Fifteen steps, twenty, twenty-five—my fingers hit a raised slat with rounded edges. Another door.

I slide my shoes back on and search for the handle. Grab hold and push.

The click rockets through the quiet, hinges creaking as light spills in. Not much—faint and dirty, but enough. Which means there are windows.

And a door.

I RUN.

I don't know where I am.

Dark skytowers crowd the streets. The night is thick, the thoroughfares narrow, and the walkways clean but cracked.

I press deep into the shadows between an alley and an awning, and try to catch my breath. My lungs burn with my legs. I don't know how many streets I've crossed, how many blocks I've come.

I don't know anything.

The city has always been home. Even before Missa gave Yonni the suite, before Yonni came and got me, before Mom left—I always lived here, in the capital. Somewhere. Different districts—hell, once even a different continental sector—but always *here*. Home.

This doesn't feel like home.

My feet have stopped, but my heart won't. Doesn't. Lungs churning on air that won't stick. I bend over double. I'm going to throw up.

"You got out," I say aloud, jarring my already jarred breath. "They had you, but you got out."

I'm clear.

All I have to do is find a street sign, and if I don't know it, walk to the next one.

This street is commercial. Dark shopfronts with pale, sloped awnings that flutter in the nonexistent breeze like ghosts. Above them, tower floors rise level after level in cycglass and crisscross steel, up into the night. It's full dark, no moon.

We left the boarding tower early in the afternoon, me, Greg, and the power tech.

I need to find the power tech.

Greg, I need to kill.

But first the power tech, in case he's dead.

"Come on," I tell myself. "Come on."

My body grumbles but gets its shit together. Eases into a rhythm that won't make me implode. I straighten, brush myself off, pick a direction, and walk.

THEY SAY ALL ROADS LEAD TO THE HOUSE ARCHIVE.
They're right.

I didn't recognize the street two blocks over, but I know this space. This empty block of sky amid a wealth of towers. A gap tooth of quarantined rubble. The city put big sliding fences up to hide the view, but everyone knows what it looks like. We saw the newsfeeds.

I felt the explosion. I was on my way home. Mom had just given me the grand tour of her lab, where she worked in House-wide data storage and manipulation, and then scent mapping on the side.

She'd been normal, as normal as I knew her to be after a month of slow lunches at cafés or in parks. Assured, concise, with that deceptively open air. She seemed confident, trustworthy, had worked her way up to being one of the lead Archivists with—she said—unparalleled security access. She'd spent most of that last night looking at me.

Then she'd given me her bracelet, cupping my hands between her cool ones to blow one hot breath into our palms.

You've the whole world, remember? Mom said, smiling. *What will you do with it?*

I opened my mouth and her smile grew.

And don't say 'give it back,' she said.

I said it anyway.

She kissed my temple. The first and only time she kissed me that I remember.

Then she sent me home and bombed the datacore of our House.

Light tubes burn along the fence surrounding the space where the Archive was, bright enough to pick out the pockmarks in the street. Cast harsh shadows under the hats of the City Enactors, even as the light shows off their shiny boots. The guards walk the circumference, stopping at intervals, keeping watch.

I pull back into an alley before they get too close. *Kreslyn Franks returns to the scene of her mother's crime* is not a story I want to read.

At least I know where I am.

Home lies between me and the boarding tower. I swing the extra three blocks out of the way. I need a bathroom and a shower and a change of clothes. It has to be past midnight, maybe later. Whatever has happened to the power tech will have happened by now. Another half hour won't hurt. Just as long as I don't sit down.

If I sit, I'll crash.

I pass through West 1st's shopping district with its broken windows and barred doors, and round the corner to my street. My tower slides into view. Squat and boxy, the forgotten stepchild of its taller neighbors. I haul myself up the cracked steps and press my keypass to the security panel.

The door clicks and I'm home.

I hit the stairwell. It takes forever, making my feet rise, but I manage. Five floors later and I'm at my door.

It's ajar.

Dad.

My keypass slips from my slack fingers, and I bolt into the suite. The couch is empty, the curtains drawn, the place dark.

I told him to be here. He said he'd be here.

Which means the Brinkers got here before me. I've been walking in circles, but they knew where to go.

A cry from my room, a groan, a growl. The door half-closed.

Dad.

I grab one of Yonni's empty vases from the couch side table—a sleek metal cylinder and heavy as hell—and inch toward my room on quiet feet. Press the door open with silent fingertips. Heft the vase.

Naked. They're naked. My bed is piled with naked people. A dark-haired breasty woman—no, a dark-haired breasty *Annie* from level four—astride some sandy-haired guy with stringy limbs and—

"That's my girl," says a voice I've known since birth.

I drop the vase. It thuds. They don't hear.

I run.

Out the door, down the stairs, through the lobby. Out into the muggy night with its muggy air that fizzes down my throat and expands into knots.

In my bed. He was in my *bed*. I saw him, saw his—oh god. I rub hard at my eyes but the image won't scrub out. Emblazoned in sweaty neon.

Oh god.

I sink, collapse onto the outer steps. Curl over my knees until my arms hang near my toes. "Bastard," I whisper. The empty street doesn't answer and doesn't care. "Bastard."

With *Annie* of all people. Someone from my building and whom Mrs. Divs likes. Who can't be that much older than me. And when Dad switches from screwing to screwing her over, they'll be two more people in the world who hate my guts. Because obviously, if I hadn't let him in, none of this would have happened.

In my bed. In *Yonni's* bed. I wouldn't put much of anything past Dad, but hell, even I wouldn't have thought—

I laugh. Or choke.

Idiot. I am such an idiot.

My stomach wants to upend my guts, but there's nothing to heave. I haven't eaten since—I can't even remember.

I knock my head against my knees.

Get up.

I will get up and get Dad's ass dressed. Then he'll not only escort me to the boarding tower, he'll share a room with the power technician and nurse him back to health or consciousness or whichever's required.

My muscles refuse, fight every attempt to stand. Finally I press both fists to the cracked steps and force myself upright. My legs will either work, or I'll dive headfirst down the stairs. They work.

I climb to the door and dig in my back pocket for my keypass. Then in my side pocket. Then pat myself down all over.

Nothing.

I dropped the pass on the floor of my suite.

"God dammit." I slap the door, but it doesn't magically open. Stupid, I am so damn *stupid*.

I am not buzzing Dad to let me into my own suite.

Not that he'd even hear. Bastard.

I scan the thin digiscreen embedded above the entrance intercom, with its rotating list of names and apartment numbers.

Mrs. Divs would buzz me, but I'd have to wake her. She doesn't need that. Nobody needs that. Certainly not any of the other names I can't match to faces, despite having seen them around.

The list cycles in order through the floors. Ten, one, two—three.

Niles Ryker, 308.

Our dinner.

I stood him up.

My forehead drops to the intercom box as the list cycles to the next floor.

He's going to kill me.

But at least I didn't kill myself in the process, so he can't say I don't keep my word.

I didn't keep my word to Yonni about Dad.

I slap the wall, hard—rough, grating stone that scrapes my wrist and doesn't care. *I* don't care. I absolutely do not care.

Any second now, I'll bawl.

I plug in the suite number and hit the intercom.

Several long seconds, then the speaker barks a tight "Yeah?"

"Niles?"

Silence. "Kit?"

"I locked myself out. Can you—"

The door buzzes open.

"I'm sorry," I say, but the speaker's dead. I push inside and retrace the endless, twisting climb to my level.

Niles waits outside my suite. Same outfit as this morning, same rumpled hair, but different. Less sexy, more tired, and tense.

My door stands open, and through it float the duel moans of round two.

Or three. You never know with Dad.

Niles glances from the door to me, and for once there's no smile in him. He stares long enough at my legs that I look, too. My pants are ripped. Climbed out a busted window getting away from the Brinkers.

A crash from my suite. Breathy laughter. A giggled squeal.

My bones frost, my face heats, and I fist my fingers until they crack. "Sorry to wake you. Thanks for letting me in."

I move, but Niles slides between me and the door.

"That your dad?" Niles asks. "I thought you kicked him out."

"I'm about to." I try to bypass him, but he locks his arm across my doorway.

I close my eyes and manage not to scream. "Please, can you just—"

"I'll get him out," he says.

"What?"

We're very close and even the soft curve of his face can't belie the underlying determination.

"Do you want him in there?" he asks.

"No, but—"

Another shriek, a second crash. What the hell are they breaking?

"Do you really want to walk in on that?" Niles asks, soft.

The heat in my face centers in my eyes. I look away and squeeze them tight. I'm not going to cry.

"Besides, you look like hell," he says.

"Thanks for the heads-up."

"Here." He presses something thin and flat into my palm. A keypass. "I'll meet you at my place."

"It's not your job, and he's naked," I say, already cracking.

"That, I figured." He gently takes my shoulders and turns me toward the elevator. "Go before you fall over."

I shouldn't. I really, really shouldn't.

But stupidity seems to be my thing, so I do.

NILES'S SUITE, OR RATHER HIS GRANDFATHER'S, IS smaller than mine but more open. A single wide room with gray carpet, with a sterile kitchen and messy bed in opposite corners, and a couch and chair between. Only the bathroom is enclosed. I lock myself in.

Bottles scatter the sink's counter. Shaving cream, hair gel, some kind of cologne. No wonder his hair is always perfectly messy. Of course there's a trick to it. I scrub my hands and face the mirror.

I wear the whole day on my skin.

My hair frizzes out of its bun, a ghostly halo around overdark eyes and a scraped temple. Not sure when that happened. I take down my hair and comb it back into a ponytail. Better.

I wash my face and arms, clean up the scratches, brush the worst of the dirt from my clothes. I cup my hands under the faucet and steal a drink, or three. I'm as presentable as I'm going to get, and it's time to open the door. Instead, I lean into it.

What if Niles is out there?

What if he isn't?

I open the door.

Niles half sits on the back of his low couch, a glass in each hand. His smile doesn't reach his eyes. "Better?"

"Dad?"

"Gone. I even let him get dressed. Her too. Here." Niles hands me a glass and thumps the ridge of the couch cushion with his knuckles. "Have a seat."

I sniff the drink. Sweet, but spiked. Not brandy, something lighter. "To drown my sorrows?"

"Would you rather have water?" He stands, moves toward the kitchen. "Don't have much else."

I shake my head. Dad lives his life wasted, why can't I?

The digiclock in the kitchen says it's after three.

I sink into the couch, but instead of joining me, Niles pulls the chair opposite closer. We face each other, knees almost brushing.

An interrogation then.

He sets his drink aside. I down mine in one gulp. It slides easy and burns a little, a harsh, radiating quiet.

Niles gapes.

I stare into my glass. "What . . . was that?"

He eyes me like any second I'll burst into flames. "Uh, sweetblue."

So, lighter than brandy, but stronger than wine. Definitely stronger. And I can't remember when I last ate. Lovely.

Too late now.

I set my glass on the table and hug my arms. "Okay. Have at me."

"What?"

"The questions," I say. "Reprisals, whatever. Shoot."

He blinks, lips stuck open. Apparently, I'm saying all the wrong things today. He stares and stares, and stares some more.

I know I don't look that bad.

My chest knots and my eyes heat, and this sweetblue is freakin' worthless.

"You okay?" Niles asks.

"You're the one who dealt with Dad; how are you feeling?"

"Fantastic. You?"

"Over the moon."

He smiles with more warmth, though still no laughter— that constant, teasing undercurrent in every subtle look. Funny how blinding warmth is once it's gone. "You're pretty scraped up. Get in a fight?"

Now that he mentions it, my stomach cries murder from a fist-size bruise. I hug my waist and fight the urge to double over. "Don't remind me."

The smile disintegrates and he leans forward, elbows on knees, serious now. "You *were* in a fight."

"No. One punch isn't a fight, it's just—" I reach for my glass, but it's empty. I set it back down. "I don't know. I got out."

"Out?" His voice lowers like it did in the hall, registers with the hum in my blood. "From where?"

"I don't know, okay? I don't know where I was." I grab the edge of the couch cushions, arms straight at my sides. But the dark's lodged in my head now, along with the slide of the calm one's hand down my spine. His easy assurance, his assumption of right. They hadn't *intended* to dose me, so, of course, it doesn't matter if I—

"The power tech." I bolt upright. The room spins, but it doesn't matter. "Hell."

Niles is on his feet, chair burning the carpet as he kicks it back, so there's room enough for him and me. "What—"

"You don't understand. Greg dosed him before he dosed me. And now the residents have probably robbed him blind and the clerk kicked him out, and—"

"Wait." He takes my shoulders as I sway, the room refusing to steady. "Somebody dosed you?"

I reach for the small bump on my neck, then let my hand fall. "Doesn't matter. I have to go."

His eyes narrow and he gathers my hair over my opposite shoulder to bare the area I'd touched. Closes in, peering, neck craning to see, until my nose is practically in his hair.

His scent has layers. Open with undercurrents. Like the city up high, at night on the rooftop, but more . . . boy.

Probably the stuff from his bathroom counter. The gel or the cologne. Except—I close my eyes and breathe. Nothing astringent, there's too much depth. A subtle core. A reality. I want it to be real.

It's not, or probably isn't, but if it was—

Maybe he'd taste of it, too.

His thumb brushes my neck where the needle bit and I jerk, jarring us both.

"Shit, sorry," he breathes, and I feel that, too. Against my neck. Down my back. Even my toes light up. He pulls away and flicks at his hair with an irritated shake, leaving the full brown-black of his eyes front and center. "Who was it? Who dosed you?"

I close my eyes to hide his. Focus.

The sweetblue isn't helping.

Niles isn't helping.

"The power technician," I repeat, almost chant in my head. "I have to find him. They said Greg didn't kill him, but that's not exactly proof. They said a lot of things."

"Kit?" A perfect balance of *K* and *T*. Everyone always overemphasizes one or the other. "What's going on?"

"Nothing. Not your problem."

"If it's nothing, then tell me." He's too near, especially with the couch at my back and nowhere to go. Not that I want to go anywhere.

"Wasn't Dad enough for one day?" I ask.

"Won't know until you tell me."

"What do you care?"

He halves the distance between us without actually touching. That shouldn't be possible. "You buzz my door in the middle of the night with your face scraped up, your clothes half-torn and a hole in your neck. Call me curious."

And you stood me up, he doesn't add.

I shake my head. "I shouldn't have buzzed you."

"That's *not* what I meant."

"Then what did you mean?"

His bangs fall again, and he swipes them back with frustrated fingers. "What the hell is going *on*?"

"I got grabbed, okay? My cousin set me up."

"Your cousin?"

I sigh. "I'm sure they paid him well."

He starts to say something, stops, and instead reaches for my neck, hand hovering an inch from my skin. "Can I?"

He is heat even without contact, a gravitational force. My nerve endings cluster below his palm. If I were smart, I'd say no.

So, of course, I nod.

His hand is light, fingers skimming the puncture like he can't believe it's there. Except every pass underlines its existence. Proof that, yep, Greg did that. The same Greg who used to plan adventures into abandoned towers, and taught me to love rooftops in the first place.

"Who paid him?" asks Niles quietly.

"Brinkers. The kids from the market. You remember the girl with the knife? They want something from Mom."

His hand goes still. "Your mom."

I grin, except my lips don't want to twist the right way. "Yeah. Apparently, she's alive—and a god, by the way—and they need her for—their home or something." Which is beside the point. All of this is beside the point, which is, "They fed Greg a line, and so he dosed this power tech before he dosed me, and now the tech's probably lying unconscious somewhere, because I'll bet no one shot him with Clarity to wake him up."

Niles blanks out.

"That's how the Brinkers woke me," I say. "It's an anti-doser. It's supposed to be regulated, or at least it was when Greg—" *Was dealing*, I don't say, because there's no way in hell I'm having *that* conversation.

Niles is still a blank slate. My explanation must suck. I don't know that I care. My head hums and my blood buzzes, and I'm losing time.

"I have to go."

"Now?" Niles glances at the kitchen's digiclock. "It's three thirty."

"I told you, I have to make sure the power tech isn't dead."

That my cousin didn't kill someone. That he hasn't become Mom.

I remove Niles's hand from my neck and don't—do *not*—wrap my fingers through his. Instead, I squeeze between him and the couch into cold open space.

The floor tips into the walls. I lock my knees, reach for the back of Niles's chair—and get him instead. His arm wraps my waist. Solid, bare. I turn, which puts us chest to chest, his hand splayed on my back. "Seriously, Niles—"

"I'll find him," he says. "Give me a description and tell me where. It shouldn't be hard—if he's dosed he's probably still down."

What?

Niles would—*what*?

I mouth the word but can't get it out. Nothing sticks. And it gets worse the more his lips quirk, skirting a smile, *his* smile. The real one, hidden and hinted and all the way to his eyes.

He winks. "Trust me, I'm good at this shit."

"No, you can't go and—you don't even know him! Hell, *I* don't even know him."

He shrugs. "Well, there you go."

"That's not—don't be stupid!"

His grin hits, full tilt, both arms squeezing tight as he leans back and lifts me.

My toes hang, dangle. I lay anchored to his chest.

"But it's fun being stupid," he says.

I clutch his shoulders. The room swishes with my feet, but his face keeps focus. Cheeks wide with his warm mouth, under laugh-scrunched eyes.

How could traipsing through the city in the dark make anyone cheerful?

"Why?" I ask.

"I told you."

"Niles."

"We're both from the neighborhood. Gotta stick together."

"*Niles.*"

He grows serious. "I'm sober, you're not. You can't even stand without weaving—not that that's stopped you." He straightens, his hold relaxing. I slide, feet reclaiming the floor by inches, heart scattering beats against his chest. His smile scatters with them, catching on a whisper. "And maybe I'm only so much of an asshole."

"You're not an asshole," I say.

"Yeah." Unassured, disbelieving, fingers snagged in my shirt even as he slides back to give me space. His lips snag, too—pale, full, and catching the light. Soaking it in. "Do you want to crash here? Your dad really did a number on—"

I lean forward to see if he tastes like his smile. He freezes, then pulls back just as my lips reach his. Almost jerks.

The air tastes acidic, empty. His arms disentangle, and I'm alone.

So neighbors who stick will kick out dads and search for strangers, but they don't kiss.

Or else they don't kiss me.

"It's late," he says.

I hug my chest and feel his. "And I thought this day couldn't get worse."

He flinches. "Kit—"

"Skip it." I walk toward the door without tripping. Mostly. Amazing what a steel ball in your gut will do.

Niles reappears my side. "I'm sorry, I shouldn't have given you that sweet—"

"Find the technician and we'll call it even. Here." I stop and dig in my pocket for my transaction card. "I'll give you the reds for his board."

Not like Dad needs them, he can stay with Annie.

The card isn't in my right pocket, so I try my left. My back pockets, the low side one.

Then I try them all again.

And again.

"What's wrong?" Niles asks.

I smile. A real smile, that slips into a laugh. Then I'm doubled over, giggling, my chest ripping apart.

"Kit?" High and wary, like I'm some alien thing.

"They took it," I gasp.

He stares.

"My transaction card. Those stupid—"

Except it wasn't the Brink kids. I'd bet all the reds I don't have.

It was Greg.

I choke. Fall to my knees with the shreds of my soul.

This is what I get for selling Yonni out. My just reward.

Niles crouches close, hand on my shoulder. "Kit?"

"You know I pawned Yonni's pendant? The heart one that she loved? Used it to clear Dad with Decker, so Dad wouldn't end up as dog bait." Another favorite method of Decker's for clearing debts. "I even got enough reds over to cover his room at the boarding tower."

Niles squeezes a half beat. "That's what this morning was about?"

I sit back on my heels to stare at the ceiling. "I had to clear it somehow, and I don't have a job."

Except, yes I do. Mr. Remmings called this morning. Yesterday morning. Maybe the whole day wasn't wasted. Worthless.

I'll take anything.

"Just cover the tech's room for tonight," I say. "I have a shift in—" I glance at the clock. Oh god. "About five hours, and I'll pay you back."

"No, you won't," says Niles. "Only so much of an asshole, remember? I'll cover it."

"You're not an asshole," I tell the floor.

He shakes his head and stands. "Say that when you're sober."

ELSE

T
HE WALLS PRESS IN AROUND YONNI'S SKINNY
glass bed, heavy and gray. Metallic to match its
metallic scent. A little sweet, a little burnt. The large
slat of a headboard, coated in digiscreens and readouts, whirrs
and blinks and monitors the tubes.

My mother sits across the way, chair balanced on its two
back legs. She holds a datadisc high over her head, between
her thumb and forefinger, shifting as if to block the ceiling
light.

Yonni lies peaceful in bed, seems to have more color. The
reprieve before the end.

"Funny how the small things are often the strongest," she
says. "Maybe it's the surprise, the power of the unexpected.
You were unexpected."

"You mean getting pregnant?" I ask. It's warm in the
room, and I've sat here a long time, forever, and still Mom
stays. I don't get it.

"That too." Mom sighs. "I was very young."

This is probably where I should say, "It's all right."

I don't.

"But I was thinking of your marching into my office," she says. "Out of the blue after how many years? Ten? I never thought to see you again, and there you were—a force of nature. So much power in your hands, and you didn't even know." She clutches the datadisc in a tight fist. "You scared me. I'd forgotten what that feels like."

And here, I probably should apologize, but I don't. I'd meant to be scary. Yonni needed meds—high-end, experimental. Dee wouldn't help me, Greg had disappeared, and Dee wouldn't say where, and Decker had laughed me from the room. I'd had no money and no help, and the only person who could offer both had dumped me when I was eight.

"Would you really have told everyone about my connection to the Accountants if I hadn't paid for the treatment?" she asks.

"Yes," I say.

I'd have screamed it from the rooftops.

I sit up, back straight, chest pounding. Bittersweet metallic in my nose and on my tongue, but this isn't the medical room. It's my room. The floor of my room. The carpet brushes soft under my fingers, scattered in blankets and pillows. Yonni's thin wooden nightstand tipped sideways on the floor. Her bed looms crooked, caved in.

Oh. Right.

My head's hollow, brain rattling as I scrub my face and take in the broken mess of my bedroom. I'd left the lights off last night, curled up on the floor. Knowing Dad, he probably started on the couch first.

No, don't go there.

I push my hair from my eyes and crawl over to the bed. Pull the dangling sheet off the rest of the way. A long crack splinters the wood frame all the way down.

Way to go, Dad.

The sheet reeks of sweat and sex. I ball it up and there, on the floor where the fabric pooled, lies my Gilken digibook.

The screen's cracked.

I drop the sheet for the slate. Press the thin power button on the outer edge. It's sticky. The whole screen's sticky and busted. It doesn't light up.

"Come on." I lift my finger and press the button again, and again. "Please. *Please.*"

This edition was a one-time manufacture. They don't make it anymore. It's annotated. A full digital collection with rare, unpublished articles. It was a one-time thing.

I sold Mom's bracelet with Yonni's heart. I have nothing else of Mom's—nothing that she gave me, that she owned. Everything else was lost or sold.

The Gilken book was all I kept, and now it's a spiderweb of gaps.

So am I. Can't even find his words in my head. None that fit.

I sink to my heels.

"Really?" Mom asked, when she found out where I worked. *"So you did read that old digibook I got you. Did you apply to the museum because of that?"*

Yes.

"No," I said, straight into her eyes.

A high melody chimes through the room. Yonni's favorite songbird clock, tumbled on the floor with its nightstand perch. Busted wing, cracked beak, its large digit eyes blink from 6:59 to 7:00.

Early tours at the Gilken Museum start at eight, and it's a good forty-minute walk.

I grab my uniform from the closet, a sleeveless knee-length green dress with alternating blocks of purple and blue at the hem. Green for the Gilken Museum, blue and purple signifying me as an official House employee. The colors echo in the faint glow of the medallion pinned high on the upper right breast.

Kit Franks, reads the small digiscreen planted between the medal's blossomed vines. *Information Guide.*

I scrub myself raw in the shower, rush through makeup and the disaster of my hair.

Yonni was into scarves. Loud, glittery, flamboyant. I

dig through the closet for the one that screams least—blue, yellow, and pink dotted—pull my hair tight and wrap my head. It takes some finagling to fold the worst of the color out of the way, but in the end it works. The dress shows off my hips, the scarf trails neatly over my shoulder, the makeup covers the worst of my undereye circles. I look . . . almost human.

I stand straight and smile for the mirror.

An awful, gutted smile.

I exhale and try again.

"Welcome to the Gilken Museum, where the official record of our House was born."

The words come easy, airy, backed by a hundred happy repetitions. My reflection follows, relaxing into habit. Face, posture, tone. "Gilken first began his quest to create what we now know as the Archive's datacore in the basement of an old digiwatch repair shop, which is where we'll begin ours. Mind your step."

She's assured, the girl in the mirror. Bright and sleek. Pretty, well-versed, can pull out a quote with the snap of a finger.

She's even kissable. Very kissable, I would have thought.

My stomach twists, and I flatten both hands on the counter. The reflection cracks, poise lost. She aches inside and out. Eyes shadowed, chin set. But it is set. Her shoulders too. Set to keep the breaks from spreading, but still. There's a strength to her.

It's the primary law of practical courage, Gilken once said, in one of his more famous political commentaries. *Surviving the weakest base means graduating from the strongest school.*

That particular quote gave the Prime Enactor his title.

Yeah, well. Time to test it.

Past time. The songbird flashes seven twenty-two.

The living room continues the bedroom's mess, bottles and glasses. I ignore it. Move straight into the kitchen to grab my backup transaction card from its spot behind the PowerFlakes box—Yonni always put stuff there—and my keypass from the counter. The card's empty, but this way Mr. Remmings can pay me for my shift.

I lock up the suite and skip the elevator for the stairs. Hit the lobby at a run.

"Kit!" calls a high, rickety voice.

I skid, narrowly missing Mrs. Divs's outstretched cane. She's in bright gold today, with a big floppy hat and fuzzy slippers. She always wears slippers, even when it's baking.

She ticks a wrinkled finger. "How many times have I told you about running in the lobby?"

"I know, I'm sorry," I say. "I'm late."

"Can't be worth giving yourself a heart attack over. Now come here, I want to talk to you."

"I can't, Mrs. Divs. Not now."

"Yes, now." She lifts her cane and points it at her open door. "In."

"I'm on shift." I try to inch around her, but like all the ancient, she's surprisingly spry when she wants to be.

She slides her tiny gold self into my path. "Don't lie to me, girl. I know you got fired." She presses her finger into my uniform medallion. "And don't think this fools me for a minute."

"My boss called me in." And if I'm any later, there's no way I'll ever get my job back—prior perfect track records notwithstanding. Mr. Remmings doesn't tolerate excuses. "We'll talk after; I'll come right back." I step forward.

Her cane smacks my thighs and her voice drops. "I saw your mother on the feeds yesterday."

I freeze. Mom. The double power-out.

You will be held to Account.

The feed must have gone out of district to reach here. Maybe even planetwide. Mom's face on every screen.

I'd forgotten. How the hell could I *forget*?

Mrs. Divs nods, secure in her hit. "Now, I can be your Guardian Sun and *not* tell the Records Office what your dad's been up to, or you can march on out of this building and face the consequences."

Breath disappears, words a whisper. "Please, Mrs. Divs."

She pats my cheek. "Two can play this game, dear one."

Without her, I won't have a place to live if Dee gets chatty.

Without a job, I can't afford to live, period.

"Mrs. Divs, I swear—"

"Mornin', Mrs. Divs!" Happy, laughing.

Niles.

My face flames and my hands fist.

Weakest base. Strongest school.

"Why, Niles!" Mrs. Divs's expression lifts, whole demeanor changing. "Where have you been keeping yourself? I haven't seen you in an age!"

"Aw, come on Mrs. D. It's only been a day and a half."

He slides in beside us, fresh and put together. Hair combed, slacks sharp, shirt crisp with buttons. Not quite a suit, but close enough. The fabric glides with his frame as he leans forward to kiss Mrs. Divs's cheek.

She beams. "Now, where you off to all fancied up?"

"Takin' Kit to work and making a hash of it." He throws me a grin. "Sorry, I'm late."

I don't say anything.

Mrs. Divs's cane magically disappears. "Oh, so that boss of yours *did* call? How very grand. Off with you, then!" Her mouth takes on its *no nonsense* line as she looks at me. "And, of course, you'll come *right back*."

"Of course," I say as Niles jogs to the lobby door and holds it open.

"After you," he says.

"DID YOU FIND THE POWER TECH?" I ASK AS WE HURRY down the entrance steps. I hurry. Niles keeps pace. "Was he still in the alley?"

He laughs. Not a happy laugh, hands thrust deep in his pockets.

I stop midstep. "Oh God, don't tell me he's dead."

"He's fine, just a little preoccupied about your mom's feedshow. Wouldn't shut up about it. Don't know why you were worried, he certainly wasn't about you."

"Oh." I hug my arms. "Well, at least he's not dead."

His lips part, form a word or thought, but he thinks better of it.

I have no business looking at his stupid lips.

I kick the cracked pavement. "I'm guessing you saw it, too—Mom's thing. You didn't mention it."

"And when should I have brought that up? In the hall outside your suite, or after I got you wasted?"

I wince. "Right. You're right. Skip it." I take off down the street.

Niles swears and catches up. "Where are you going?"

"Work. I'm late."

He jerks a thumb over his shoulder. "Ride's this way."

"I don't have reds for transit."

"My ride. I've a hover. It's shit, but it'll get us there."

I stop. "Wait, the offer was real?"

"Of course it's real. And if we don't turn around, you will be late."

"But don't you have to be somewhere?"

"This morning? Just your work."

"But you're . . ."

"What?"

All dressed up. Why is he dressed up?

Niles jams his hands in his pockets, only to tug them back out.

"Okay," I say. "Let's go."

"YOU'RE LATE." MR. REMMINGS SWEEPS ME AWAY from the employee side door as if he'd been pacing the hall. There are no chairs to sit on this side, nothing but walls and doors. "You know when the early shift starts. I distinctly remember giving you the time."

He clips his *T*'s the way he cracks his heels, footsteps weighted heavy. He looks like a *T*—broad shoulders, slim waist, narrow legs.

"I'm early, sir."

Niles sped through the growing traffic as if his life was at stake. Or maybe just to get out of the silence. His whole focus fixed on the road, mine on the side window.

Mr. Remmings raises his wrist, shakes his cuff, and flashes an ornate digiwatch.

It backs me up.

"Five minutes hardly counts as early, Franks. Conscientious employees leave at least fifteen."

No one's met that standard as long as I've been on staff.

Assuming I'm actually on staff again.

"Does that mean I have my job?" I ask.

He doesn't bother answering, spinning on his heel to trek down the pale hall. Doors face off at intervals, between employee notice screens. Staff meetings, tour schedules, random updates. Sari finally settled on the Market for her birthday party. Trent wants to start an amateur skidball team. Mac's pissed because someone has stolen his lunch for a week straight.

For the first time, I want to stop and tap the screen. Type in: *Pack cloudcakes for lunch, then pump them full of hotspice and agen. Remember that week Denze spent puking up his guts? Trust me on this.*

Except no one would, not Millie Oen's daughter. Or for that matter, Kit Franks. I didn't circulate much. Everyone was older or in school, lived in High South or Blue East. No one came from West 1st, and no one read Gilken for the joy of it. This wasn't a dream but a job to them. I didn't fit.

But maybe I didn't try.

Mr. Remmings pauses at the last door, which leads to the museum's central lobby, and checks his watch again. We've a minute to spare. He reaches for the door handle.

"Mr. Remmings?" I ask.

He jumps. "What?"

"You know that power technician you hired? I ran into him yesterday, and he looked pretty ill." Or did after Greg got done with him. "I think he was going to the clinic, so if he doesn't call in they probably have him drugged up."

"Power technician?" Mr. Remmings asks. "What power tech?"

We just needed to talk to you without the Shadow, the Brinker had said.

The walls hem me in, my throat tight and thick and words come slow. "The one redoing the circuits on the rooftop."

"I'm not diverting funds for the lunch break haven of an employee who isn't even *employed.*" Mr. Remmings tries to loom, except he's not tall enough. "Don't assume I don't know how much time you spent up there. We're barely eking by as is. Another year like last one, and we may have to close our doors."

A Shadow. My cousin dosed an Enactor *Shadow*. The Brinkers were right.

Mr. Remmings glares and autopilot kicks in.

"No, sir," I say. "Of course not. My mistake."

Mr. Remmings leans back and straightens his jacket. "If you want to remain under our banner, you must remember that good employees are dedicated to preserving the museum above all else."

I keep my head up, shoulders back, and refuse to feel the hit. "Yes, sir."

He opens the door. "Then get to it, Franks."

I step through.

The grand lobby arcs in a perfect circle, vast and open. Staircases curve the walls between story-high windows and thin partitions complete with chairs and embedded wall-screens. Each a digistorage access point for a different historical record. Tiled stripes of green, blue, and purple spiral across the floor, radiating from the tower's central golden sun.

A small crowd stands around the sun, almost full tour capacity. An odd mix of everyday adults in work clothes. Usually our tours run on students or the historically passionate. The ancient interested in expanding their education, or simply in a way to spend an afternoon. Sometimes we'll have visitors from different planets and sectors within our House—and once I even had a couple from the House of Westlet—but not often. This city is the central core of Galton. While Scholar Gilken is among our most famous historical figures, there are other things to see.

Not today, apparently.

Behind me, the employee door clicks closed. Mr. Remmings is gone. It's just me and the fifty-plus people packing the lobby floor. Tired people with grim eyes and drawn faces.

Someone calls, "It's her," and my toes ice over.

No one's here for Gilken. They're here for a show.

And Mr. Remmings provided.

I want to turn around and walk out.

Can't.

So I walk straight into the sun. Stand not to the side or behind like I normally do, but smack in the center of the vivid tile.

"Welcome to the Gilken Museum, where the official record of our House was born."

The whole room shifts, darkens. They want to eviscerate me. They can get in line.

"Gilken first began his quest in the basement of an old digiwatch repair—"

"Really?" calls someone male, though I can't pick him out in the crowd. "That's all you've got to say?"

The shape of the group splits between those who shuffle and those who don't. But this isn't my first tour or even my worst one, at least not yet.

I don't change tone or take the bait. "Would you rather start with the fifth-level balcony, instead? And the initial research on—"

"I'd rather start with you," calls the faceless man.

Of course he would.

I make my smile stick. "As you like. I've been with the museum two years, but my fascination with Gilken began much earlier—"

"Why?" Female this time and less harsh. The crowd shifts to my right, front row rearranging to showcase a heavyset woman. Her hair is gray at the roots, round face soft, arms limp under loose sleeves. She looks ancient, a match for Mrs. Divs with her ringed eyes and weary mouth, but I don't think she's that kind of old. Closer to

Dad's age then Yonni's.

I retrace the conversation, careful to answer the exact thread. "Because Gilken always has the perfect answer. Whatever the problem, he's thought it through."

"And my daughter's passing?" asks the woman. "When they pulled her charred body out of the wreckage? What would Gilken say about that?"

Family. They're not gawkers, they're family.

He'd say I'm a stupid, careless idiot who doesn't have a heart. No wonder they want to skin me. They've earned the right.

I grab my forearm behind my back and dig my nails in. Fight the sudden need to giggle, the buckle in my knees.

Stand, I will *stand*.

"Why did she do it?" the woman asks, and the words drip even if her face doesn't. "Why did she have to involve my baby?"

Because Mom probably didn't know her daughter, and if she did, she didn't care. Nothing mattered more than the Accounting.

I certainly didn't.

"I'm sorry," I say. "I'm sorry."

Useless. No amount of "sorry" helped me when Yonni died.

The woman closes her eyes, and I can feel the tears that

don't fall. If I was Missa, I'd step forward and offer something—a hug? A shoulder?—but I'm Millie Oen's daughter and haven't that right.

"You call that an answer?" yells the man in back. "You think it's enough that—"

Something clatters. Echoes off the ringing walls and we jerk, all of us, twisting for a better view. Bodies shift, the crowd opens, and through the newly formed gaps stands Niles. Hair gone messy, shirt sleeves rolled to his elbows, eyes wide with his shocked mouth. "Aw, hell, sorry!" he says to the man kneeling on the floor at his side. There's a mess of gear on the tile, metal bits of black and gray strewn everywhere.

Niles fumbles to help and kicks a disc across the floor. "I really hope it wasn't expensive!"

The kneeling man swears in the faceless guy's voice. "Yes. It was."

"Shit, hold up!" Niles snatches a bigger boxy piece from the tech-scattered floor. "This isn't the Vidfire 9800, is it? The digirecorder all the big newsfeed stations use?" He looks up and across the crowd for half a heartbeat.

Our eyes meet.

"It is!" he continues, hitting the man with a huge enthused grin. "Aw, man, I've been saving up for one of these!"

The crowd straightens, glares finding a new target. A

growing murmur of "He's filming this?" and "I thought this was for family?" and "Who did he lose?"

I step back. No one notices. I could be out of the building before they realize I've gone.

Except they're not gawkers, they're family.

I stand, feet planted, back straight, and say, "I'm here."

But Niles makes a racket with the man's gear, and my voice is too tight. Too small.

"I'm right *here*," I yell. It ricochets, ceiling to heartbeats to floor, and I command the room. Can almost taste their shock and their growing tinge of anger. Even Niles's exasperation. *What are you doing?* he mouths.

I ignore him.

"You wanted me," I tell the crowd. "And here I am. Shoot."

The mother turns, eyes flashing, whole face set in a growl. She steps forward and socks me.

I stagger. My cheekbone screams. Dee never hit me with such strength, but then her hands were always open, not fists.

And hers didn't imprint my soul.

The woman stands frozen, hand high from the recoil, mouth open like someone paused her midfeed.

Niles jumps to his feet, steps forward. I catch his eye and mouth a harsh *Stay*. He stops.

This isn't his place. This is between me and the families.

I don't have the answers they need or the people they lost.

I only have me.

I straighten, lock my hands behind me, and brace for the next blow.

The woman looks at her hand, the open-palmed emptiness of it, the soft fingers that belie strength. She lifts her head. I hold her gaze, but that feels like a challenge so I switch to the floor.

The woman wears practical shoes. Brown and low heeled, laced tight. They peek from under gray, practical slacks. Maybe her daughter's shoes were practical as well. Maybe they were vibrant.

I hold my breath. Fight the scream, the waxing panic, the needles in my feet.

The waiting hurts.

She hurts worse.

Her hand falls to her side. I look up. The light catches in her too-shiny eyes. "You're a baby, too, aren't you?"

"No," I say.

Today, I'm ancient.

"I can't do this." She turns and pushes through the crowd. Jerky steps and squeezed elbows. Her back a silhouette against the aching protest of the outer door, and then she's gone.

The crowd's fire goes with her, its spirit caught in her wake. Our silence a shuffle of fabric and feet.

Everyone dissipates, files out, even the man with the busted gear. Niles skirts the crowd's shifting edges. He doesn't pause or say a word, just takes my hand and pulls.

"THAT WAS A SETUP." NILES BURNS HIS STREETHOVER around corners and down thoroughfares. "A goddamn publicity stunt. You know how expensive that digirecorder was? I'm serious about the newsfeed stations, I've seen their gear. How they'd know you'd be—"

"Mr. Remmings," I say.

Good employees are dedicated to preserving the museum, and what better way to generate income? I'm sure somebody paid him. He was never going to hire me back.

And my daughter's passing? When they pulled her charred body out of the wreckage? What would Gilken say about that?

"Your boss set you up?" Niles asks.

"Skip it." I lean into the heat of the open window, hold the ends of Yonni's scarf so it doesn't blow away.

Niles's tiny streethover predates Mrs. Divs and has her taste in color. A tacky gold box with big windows, few curves and little heft. A strong gust could blow us away.

"No, *this* we don't skip," Niles nearly shouts. "Someone must have tracked down all those families to pull this job. Do you have any idea how bad things could have gone? God, when you just stood there—"

"You can stop yelling anytime."

"I'm not yelling!"

I catch his gaze as we pause at an intersection and raise a brow.

He rolls his eyes. "Fine. I'm yelling."

Traffic clears and he jumps us forward, anger humming with the engine. But with the windows down his hair is a mess, and windswept does not invoke rampage.

"What are you smiling about?" he snaps.

"What smile?" I so wasn't smiling.

"This is serious," he says.

"I know."

"Do you?" Niles swings down a side street, where bulky residential towers glower above tiny well-kept shops. The fringes of Low South before it turns into grime. Niles pulls along the curb outside a pet shop, powers down the engine, and stares out the window.

We sit in silence.

"What if she'd been somebody else?" he asks.

"Who?"

"The one with the daughter. What if she'd been the kind who didn't stop?"

"Then she wouldn't have stopped."

And I'd have a lot more bruises.

Outside, the pet shop sports a digitized window with a digitized puppy. Its neon ears bounce with its wagging tail. It wriggles and rolls happily across the glass for ten whole seconds, its world an open possibility.

Then the loop repeats.

"You don't get it," Niles says. "There were fifty-eight people in that group. If even half joined in . . . I'd have got you out, but it would have been bad."

"No." I face him. "You don't get in the middle of that. You don't ever—"

"You think I'd just stand by and watch?"

"I think your mother didn't kill their kids, and it's not your fight." The words come gritty.

Niles leans in, blocks out the street. "Was that what that was? A fight?"

I cross my arms and don't answer.

His reaches for my jaw, light fingers at odds with his biting glare. "You're going to have a helluva shiner."

"So what? Is my health more important than their hurt?"

"Who even thinks that way?" He glances from my cheek to me.

I straighten. Put us nose to nose so he'll back the hell up. "And how am I supposed to think?"

He doesn't move an inch. Stares back with brown-black eyes and parted lips that forgot to close. His palm slides along my jaw, fingertips brushing my ear, breath rising on an upbeat. Mine is almost gone. It wouldn't take much to kiss him. I'd barely have to move.

"No," I say, but there's no air.

His "What?" comes near as soundless.

I pull away, far away, press into the passenger side.

His hand lifts, hovers where I was. "Kit?"

"No." Stronger now. "Been here, done that, got it the first time."

I yank open the door, slam out of the hover, and take off down the street.

Two beats and his door echoes mine. "Kit!"

"*Stop.*"

I swing around. He skids to a halt an arm's length away. The sun picks out his hair and cheekbones, the round tip of his nose.

"If you're going to kiss me, *kiss* me. Otherwise I don't care how nice you are—hands off. It's not a game. I'm not a game."

Even if my skin has mapped the shape of his fingers and wants them back. *Especially* since I want him back.

I turn and head for home. Not two steps later, his hand catches mine.

Apparently, the boy has a death wish.

And I am not going to bawl.

"Niles," I growl.

"Just to clarify." He swallows and steps closer. "The kissing's okay?"

"What?"

Another step, his half smile shaky and wholly un-Niles-like. "Assuming I get my shit together, a kiss would be fine?"

Oh yeah.

No.

I don't know.

"Depends." I can't meet his eyes, so I stare at his lips—like that's less dangerous. The upper one is a little uneven, lower one almost too full.

"On what?" he asks.

He is very, very close.

"Will it mean something?"

Because that matters. It didn't last night, but it does now. Except it mattered then, too.

His free hand brushes my unbruised cheek, thumb finding the corner of my mouth. "That's what scares me."

"You're scared?" It's impossible to see his face as a whole. He is skin and undercurrents, clarity and heat.

"Terrif—" he whispers, except his mouth presses soft and close.

Or else it wasn't a whisper to begin with.

He tastes like him. Niles. Careful, measured intent and contradictions. Messy assurance, sliding smiles. Laughter that lives in his lips, on his tongue, warming even when it isn't there. His palm slides along my back. I wrap my arms around his neck. My dress bunches with his fingers, his collar crinkled under mine, and every breath I snatch, he steals.

The world explodes in horns. A horn. A single street-hover wailing past.

We jump, percussion and jitters, and I press my face to his neck.

"Yeah, yeah." Niles glares after the streethover, then squeezes me tight. "Want to get breakfast?"

I smile into his skin. "What is it with you and breakfast?"

"Best meal of the day."

I raise my head. "But isn't it lunch . . . time . . ."

Something's wrong with the pet shop behind him. I lean past his shoulder for a better view.

The digital puppy is gone, replaced by Mom's soft smile. She looks right at me. Even the low-grade window-screen catches the full spectrum of her eyes, their woven brown and gray. The perfect red of her lipstick. She only wore red to work; normally she favored brown. She told me that once.

Niles kisses my jaw. I feel it; it registers. My face must be working.

I can't speak.

Neither does Mom. Her lips move, but nothing comes out.

The window isn't digitalized for sound.

"Kit?" Niles leans back, sees my face, and spins. I'm behind his shoulder, his arm a barrier between me and her.

Then he swears.

"I can't hear her," I say.

He jogs forward and rubs his hand over the glass. Searches for a control point, a switch, a button. Maybe her soul.

She blinks.

"No speakers." He slams the window with his palm.

Her face blitzes, fuzzed by the reverberation.

"No!" I tug him back and take his spot.

She's here, right here. Under my fingertips, cheek smearing shimmers with each light drag. Her lips move, and I mimic their shape with my own.

"Ends," I whisper.

Niles steps close. "What?"

I ignore him to sound out her words. "I have . . . tears—things, but rest—this . . . mystery, mine? They say good—good what?—three, but I really relieve—believe? In four."

Mom cups her empty hands, raises them to her lips, and blows.

My palms tingle.

She says something else. It ends in *heart*.

Mine cracks.

"No," I say.

The image fizzes, pops. The puppy returns, flopping ears and wagging tail.

"NO!" I slam the window twice as hard as Niles did. The glass reverberates. "Come back! You come back! You can't leave this on me, you don't have the right." I smack the glass again and again, and then there's an arm around my waist and a solid boy at my back.

He lifts me up, my feet swinging as he backs us away.

"No!" I kick—twist, tug. His arms are steel, his chest a wall. Lips at my ear, breath in my hair. "Kit, Kit, calm down."

"Calm down!" I twist hard enough to break his hold. Or else his arms loosened. I face him. His hands don't leave my waist. "I don't have to calm down. My mother is dead and she was right *there*."

Calling me brightheart, like she used to. When I was young.

I pull free of Niles. Grab my hair and get the stupid scarf instead. I toss it to the pavement. Kick it for good measure. "They're dead." I swing round and punch the window. My bones crunch my knuckles into my elbow, and my whole arm wails. "The Archive's entire night crew. You heard. They had to pull that lady's daughter out on a stretcher."

"I know." Niles's behind me. Not tugging and lifting, just quiet and there. "I know."

"She'll never get her daughter back. She's gone."

"Yeah."

"It's not okay," I say.

"It's not your fault."

"She was my mom."

"Don't take on her sins." His arms wrap around my waist, but I am stone and don't move. "They aren't yours."

"You don't know that," I whisper.

"Yeah I do," whispered back.

I twist, flatten my palm on his chest to push him away or pull him close, I can't tell. "How?"

"Easy." He takes my face in both hands and kisses my bruised cheek, at the heart of the ache. And it weirdly feels better, like I'm some kind of kid.

I close my eyes. "Weren't you just yelling at me for that?"

"Because it was stupid as hell." His mouth skims my jaw, breath and heat. Another kiss. "And brilliant. God, you've got guts. Hell, the second time I saw you, you—" He stops.

I open my eyes. "Got in a fight over the intercom and blackmailed my aunt? Yeah, that was great."

His face is quiet, skirting a blankness that almost takes over but doesn't. "Blackmail?"

"I have shit on my cousin and threatened to use it. That's why she backed down." I twist my fingers in his shirt. "Who does that?"

His hands fall to my shoulders. "Isn't he the one who dosed you?"

"He hadn't dosed me then."

And maybe he wouldn't have at all, without the threat.

After that, Greg probably thought it an even exchange.

I sag. Release Niles's maligned shirt, try to smooth out the wrinkles. "Niles?"

His hands tighten. "Yeah?"

The question drags at my tongue, aches with my cheek, but the past is past and probably should stay there.

There's only so much damage a day can handle.

I step away from him. "We should go."

"Kit." Tight and clipped. He stands very straight, arms listless. "Ask me. Just ask."

Well, I guess I started this.

"What was your dad's reputation? The one he left you with?"

Niles doesn't move, doesn't blink, the question caught in the air or the grid of his brain. A closed grid behind silent eyes.

"Skip it," I say. "I wasn't trying—"

"Appropriation," he says. "I'd say embezzlement but it's not about money, though he certainly takes his cut. It's about leverage." He grins, beautiful and twisted. "And my dad excels at leverage. Think, Decker."

My jaw drops. "He's not—?"

"No. Not him." Niles jams his hands in his pockets and

he looks away. "And just so we're clear? I'm pretty damn good myself. Even outclassed Dad a time or—"

I reach for his neck, step close and kiss him. Taste his surprise, his stillness, hesitant lips belied by the hand at my hip, grasping for anchor. A brief kiss, nothing special.

It shouldn't be this hard to breathe.

"I thought we didn't take on sins?"

"Oh lord," and he's breathless, too, forehead pressed to mine. "Don't quote me. Half the stuff I say is shit."

NILES DOESN'T ARGUE WHEN I SAY I'M TIRED AND want to be alone, probably because it's the truth. He walks me to my suite, palm pressing mine in a silent *I'm here.*

Even unspoken the words bolster the landscape, give the sky some color. Command so much power . . . but not enough.

My world is preprogrammed by Mom. That last message, whatever else it was, was for me.

I smile and close Niles out of my suite. Lean against the door as his steps retreat down the hall, and wait for the stairwell door to open. I count to ten and slip down to the main level.

Mrs. Divs answers on my second knock.

She's exchanged her bright gold dress for a more sedate red robe, its draped sleeves swinging as she puts her hands on her hips. "Don't tell me you got in a fight."

"Did you see it?" I ask.

"Of course I see it, it's half down your face."

I shake my head. "I mean Mom, on the feeds."

She snorts. "Better use asking if anyone didn't see it. What is your mother up to?"

Behold the question of the hour.

"Did you record it?" I ask.

Mrs. Divs is a veritable newsfeed archive. She records everything, remembers everything.

She stomps her cane. "Now, how am I supposed to record anything with the power gone out? It was downright eerie to have that wall-screen running and nothing else on."

"But you could tell me what she said. You remember every word, don't you, Mrs. Divs? You have an ear."

I've heard her recite whole conversations verbatim.

She preens, a silky red bird. "I do, don't I?"

"There's not a soul to match you," I say.

She levels me a wrinkled glare. "Don't think I don't know what you're doin', young miss."

But still, she swings the door wide.

I slip into her white lace wonderland, and she shoos me toward the couch. I take the end closest to the big green cookie jar. I didn't have breakfast this morning, or dinner last night.

I reach out. "May I?"

She gently smacks my fingers. "It's not even half on suppertime yet! We'll have tea first, and see if you behave. Then we'll talk cookies."

I sink into the cushions, hand in my lap. "Of course, Mrs. Divs."

Satisfied, she hobbles off to the kitchen. I try to ignore the jar. Even closed, it radiates sugar. Gingercrisp and fireplum, homemade and buttery.

Yonni couldn't cook for shit, but she used to take me

to the bakery. Once a week every week, whether she had an appointment later in the evening or not. I first met Missa in a bakery. We ran into her by accident. She bought me cloud-cakes and Yonni coffee. Yonni was livid. She pulled Missa aside where I wasn't supposed to see, and said in a voice I wasn't supposed to hear, "Not a word, not a damn word. The kid doesn't know what I do."

I'd slid in by her elbow and nearly gave her a heart attack. "Uh, Yonni? I'm eleven."

She gaped at me, then snatched the cloudcake from my hand, ordered me to a chair, and banned me from sugar for a month.

I might be on a sugar ban now, the way the cookie jar taunts me. I fold my arms and stare at the wall-screen. It's muted. Some newscast plays, but not the standard House Update. The colors and logos are different, the camera panning along streets with trees—actual trees—growing between skytowers. Two boys meander the walkway, both tall, but one towering. Literally. He has to duck under low branches and the weirdly ornate signs hanging above open shop doors. Painted signs, not digitech. The letters don't move. The shorter boy tugs the other into someplace called Our Divinity. The camera hovers in their absence.

The Lord's dead, the Archive's gone, Mom just hijacked the feeds, and *this* is the news? Not Lady Galton demanding an explanation from the Prime, or the Prime pointing out how all his resources are devoted to finding the bloodling Heir. Not some minor lordling in a panic over what will happen next, or the Market Brinkers with their protest signs, but this?

The couple reappears, carrying fluffy rolls with thick icing. The camera zooms in, and it turns out the shorter of the two isn't a boy, but a round-faced girl. She raises her pastry, closing her eyes as she breathes in obviously epic levels of sugar, and bites.

I hate her.

Cups rattle in saucers, a cane scraping tile. Mrs. Divs appears from the kitchen, tray sloped dangerously, teapot skidding.

I jump up and grab it before she stains her scattered lace. "Seriously, just ask."

"I am not too old to serve my guests tea, thank you very much."

"Yeah, yeah." I set the tray on the low table and straighten the pot while Mrs. Divs eases into the couch. She pours me a cup, and it takes all my willpower not to gulp it down.

On-screen, the couple has transferred to a garden area beside the bake shop. Green trees, green grass, even green tables and chairs. The girl talks about something and sets her sticky roll down to make shapes in the air with her hands. The boy's in a hood, but he must be listening because she responds to his responses. And they must be the right responses, because she shares her pastry.

Then it hits me.

"It's a restaurant review," I say. "Or a travel show." Pre-scheduled programming to give the newsfeeds time to evaluate Mom's latest stunt. Make a plan.

Mrs. Divs glances at the screen and barks a laugh. "Travel, I'll grant you. That, my girl, is a Westlet newscast."

"Westlet?" My cup freezes halfway to my mouth. "The *House* of Westlet?"

Inter-House network boxes are expensive. More than expensive. She'd have to get a communicator and a transfeed adaptor, and together those would cost more than her suite. Hell, more than our whole tower.

She nods, smug. "And live, too."

"No," I moan. "You didn't rob somebody, did you?" I can almost see it, Mrs. Divs on the slow sneak attack, cane raised. Or worse, pulling the Poor Little Old Ancient routine on a very rich somebody. "Don't tell me you conned a lordling."

Dad tried that, once. It did not end well.

Mrs. Divs lifts the silver remote from her table, and the screen blacks out. "Of course not! It may surprise you, but my family used to have money back in the day. Quite a lot of it."

I knew that, her furniture nearly screams "heirlooms," but an inter-House box? That's another level entirely. Lordling level. Missa level.

I raise my cup and swallow my questions back with my tea. It's warm, and a little bitter.

She watches, her saucer perched between spider fingers. "Aren't you going to ask what happened?"

"Do you want me to?"

"Not particularly."

I shrug. "All right then."

Another gulp and my tea's gone. These cups are like thimbles, but snagging a refill probably won't net me a cookie.

Mrs. Divs doesn't move, a statue in a red robe and curled locks, gaze steady and cataloging.

Tea-gulping was a bad idea. I'm so not getting a cookie.

She almost smiles. "Ah, Kit. Sometimes you are very . . . reminiscent of your line."

"Dad's gone." I meet her still gray eyes. "If that's what you're asking."

She shifts somehow, her whole demeanor easing into a shrug that never quite happens. "Now that is nice to hear. A real mistake, that. Sullies the blood."

Dad was *Yonni's* blood.

I set down my cup with easy, measured grace. Otherwise, I'd slam it. "What did Mom say?"

Her eyebrows rise. "You don't know? What with her pretty face broadcast planetwide? However did you manage that?"

"Does it matter?" I ask. "Do you remember what she said?"

"Perhaps. Though since you're so interested, maybe you can tell me what she meant to say." Soft and conversational. "Especially as you were seeing so much of her."

Especially since you probably knew what she intended and didn't stop it, she doesn't say.

I sink forward, elbows on knees, fingers laced behind my head. "It wasn't want you think."

"And what would that be?"

I close my eyes. "Please, Mrs. Divs. Just tell me."

Her bony fingers crawl over and pat my shoulder. "Now then, Kit dear, you know that's not how this works."

"This?" I push upright, her hand falling away as my own rises to my hair. "What *this*? It's not a game!"

She nods at the dark wall-screen. "Well, your mother seems to think so."

"I can't help that!"

"Can't you?" Mrs. Divs lowers her cup to her lap. "Forgive me, Kit, but I do find it odd that after Yonni cursed your mother's name for absence and abandonment, the moment

Yonni's dead you run out and track the woman down."

"No, I didn't."

Her jaw sets. "Don't you come running to me for information, then turn around and lie about—"

"It was before, all right?" I say, half rising off the couch. But there's nowhere to go, and I need to know what Mom said. I sit, breathe, and lower my voice. "Yonni needed meds. I knew Mom worked at the Archive though—through one of Yonni's lovers. She'd tracked Mom down for me, because she had the resources and she was—she was kind."

She'd come to visit once, years ago, when I was a bawling mess on the couch and Yonni rocked me. I thought I'd seen Mom in the street, but it'd turned out to be a stranger, and then the tears wouldn't stop.

Two weeks later, Missa arrived with a thin digisheet of information, which she handed to Yonni with a soft, *if she ever wants to know.*

Mrs. Divs doesn't comment, not through body or expression, an ancient impartial wall.

Yonni could do that, too, listen without judgment.

"Yonni needed meds," I say, again. "Expensive meds. Mom was an Archivest at the Archive. She also used to be hooked up with the Accountants—you know, the survivors from the indie planets? The ones we gutted? It was a super secret when I was little, so I figured if her boss at the

Archive knew, she'd be fired."

"Did you tell her boss, then?" Mrs. Divs asks.

I shake my head. "Threatened to, if Yonni didn't get her meds."

"And your mother delivered?"

"Yeah." I fold my arms across my chest, fists tight against my shirt. "The only one, out of everyone, who did."

Mom took care of everything. Yonni's medication, her glass treatment bed, found the small off-grid clinic that would take care of her and allow me to stay overnight. Not that it helped. Nothing helped.

Then after, when Yonni's body was taken and it was just me alone in the room, Mom had stopped by and asked, *Does this cover my end of our bargain, or have you other demands to make?*

If I'd had a soul, it'd have screamed, but there was nothing left for me to scream with.

No, we're even, I said and walked past her out the door. I never thought I'd see her again. Then one day, months later, I opened the door and there she was.

You want to get coffee? she'd said, and after a minute, like an idiot, I'd said, *Okay.*

Infinite seconds drag.

Then Mrs. Divs straightens and crosses her ankles, cup in lap.

"'I wish I could tell you how this ends,'" she says, my mother echoing through every ancient syllable. I raise my head. "'I have my theories, but this history isn't mine to make. I've heard that good things come in threes, but I believe in fours.'" Mrs. Divs pauses a beat, her voice more her own. "And then she did something very odd. She cupped her hands together and blew into them, saying, 'The question is a matter of heart.'"

Heart. Not brightheart.

It wasn't a secret message.

Except, she'd cupped my hands just like that, that last night, as she used to when I was little.

Mrs. Divs sets aside her tea. "Now tell me, Kit, what do you think that meant?"

Last time, unlike when I was young, my hands weren't empty.

You've the whole world, remember? What will you do with it?

The bracelet.

I stare at the empty wall-screen, my wide-eyed face reflected back.

I wish I could tell you how this ends.

You've the whole world.

This history isn't mine to make.

"What did you give me?" I ask under my breath.

"You know what she meant, don't you?" asks Mrs. Divs.

"No," I say, fast, too fast.

Mrs. Divs, on the other hand, is measured and slow. "Ah, Kit. You never were much of a liar."

I jump to my feet. "Thanks for the tea."

Her cane flashes out and traps me between the couch and the coffee table. She tsks, head shaking. "I'm a little worried, dear. More than a little, truth to tell. Here's your mother talkin' about threes and fours, when once would be enough for anyone. How long you think she'll keep this up?"

I clench my fists and don't jump the table, or clatter over her delicate painted dishes. "Please, Mrs. Divs, I have no answers."

"Then maybe you best find some." She removes her cane. I cross the room in a heartbeat. As I open the door, she calls, "I hear the Records Officials will be doing a routine check of properties soon. Should be interesting."

Not unless she tells them about Dad. She'd only have to mention him in passing and I'd be on the street. No money, no food, no bed, no Yonni.

Except for the world in my empty hands, and the sins of my mother.

"You do what you think is right, Mrs. Divs," I say and close the door.

I TAKE THE STAIRS TWO AT A TIME, HANDS SHAKING
and dizzy down to my bones. I need to eat. I need that
bracelet.

If I can trace my transaction card and give it to Decker,
I'll be five hundred short—assuming he doesn't jack the
price. I'll have to do a job for him.

Which is exactly how Greg started dealing.

I'm not Greg.

I slam out of the stairwell, feet pounding the rhythm of
Mom's voice.

Good things come in threes, but I believe in fours.

Three what? Explosions? So far, we've had only one, and
only two broadcasts.

The question is a matter of heart.

Not that she had one.

I smack my keypass to the security panel and swing
through the door. It slams behind me. The room's darker
than it should be, the curtains pulled close.

The curtains were open when I left.

There are people on the couch.

I spin on my heel—don't think, don't scream—and reach
for the door.

Arms wrap me from behind, a hand on my mouth, a clamp
on my waist. Small breasts bunch at my back. A woman.

"Now," she whispers in my ear. "Don't you go screaming."

I bite her palm and twist my whole torso. She yelps and I'm free. I jump into the kitchen—she's blocking the exit—and pull one of Yonni's big carving knifes from a drawer. Yonni hated knives, I don't know why the hell we have them. It's probably dull as hell.

"Back off." I hold the knife in front of me. The blade glints. "Just back off."

The woman backs up, hands rising and ready. "You have some nerve."

"*I* have—you're in my suite! Who the hell are you?"

Across the room, the curtains *whoosh* open. A thin male figure stands dead center, silhouette swarmed by yellow dust.

"It's beautiful out there," he says in a pretty singsong. "We see glimmers of the world."

The Brinkers. The Brinkers are in my suite, and one of them is hiding.

My fingers tighten on the knife, but that will make it harder to throw. I breathe, ease up, relax my bones. Tension screams "scared," and scared screams "gut me."

I glance at my back, but the kitchen's empty and the cabinets aren't big enough for even a child to fold into.

"Where the hell is the other one?" I ask.

"Where do you think?" bites the girl.

"They caught him," the skinny one turns, floats forward. "He wasn't fast enough. He's theirs now."

"And that's on you." The girl has topknots again, pulled tight enough her skin stretches. She steps closer.

"How the hell do you figure?" I lift the knife higher. "You people dosed *me*."

She ignores this, calling over her shoulder. "Play the vid."

"If you mean Mom's latest," I say, "I've seen it."

"She said it was *a matter of heart*." The skinny kid crosses the room to lift the remote from the table, his light brown hair haloed white. "She loves us."

"Right," I say. "That's why she blew up the Archive and screwed our House."

"Yes, exactly." The skinny kid grins, a beautiful skeletal thing, then points the remote at my wall-screen. It wakes, bright enough to take on the afternoon sun.

I focus on the girl. "What the hell do you—"

"Shut up and watch," she says.

On-screen, a large purple planet hangs amid star-strewn space, dark, splashed by cloud white and sea blue. Nothing special.

Except for the floating black rectangles ringed around it.

Flight stations. A whole slew of them, spaced at even intervals around the planet's center, seamless except for a pale silver tube that winds from bottom to top. The stations look small, but they must be massive—each a fifth of the planet's height.

"You see them?" asks the skinny kid. "They eat hearts."

Every third station begins to spin. Slow at first, then gaining speed, while the stations between them glow a pale white. Then bright white, then blinding—until each glowing set of two could be a single sphere of white fire.

The fire beams straight into the planet's heart.

It melts everything—blackens the clouds, buckles the land, wrecks the seas in a twisting mass of dying color. The planet cracks all the way across. I can almost hear it scream. Can almost feel it.

Fuel. They're gutting it for fuel.

My hand lowers. "Which world is this?"

"Casendellyn," says the girl. "The last of the independent planets. I'd have thought you two old friends, seeing as it's where your mother was born."

Mom's home? I mean, I knew she was from an indie, but . . .

The newsfeeds never showed a vid.

My stomach's a sinkhole.

Galton must be held to Account, Mom would mutter to herself, working on her digislate while I sat quietly nearby, kicking my feet against the kitchen chair and wondering if she'd ever look up. I'd made a skytower out of bread. She never did. *Must. Will. They will know our loss.*

"How do you know where she was born?" I ask. The Enactors didn't. The Prime didn't—or else he did and didn't let on.

"Because we're facing the same damn thing." The girl crosses into the living room, yanks the remote from the skinny kid and points at the screen.

A new smaller planet appears, more green than purple with candy-puff cloudscapes. Three flight stations ring its horizon to the left, one to the right, an empty gap in the middle. Far in the corner of the screen, deep in the dark stars, lies the outline of another.

"Casendellyn was thirty years ago," says the girl, "but this? Last week. While you've been jacking around playing hard to get, they've moved all the stations in place but two."

The skinny kid moves close to the screen, hands splayed on its edges, nose brushing the clouds. He sings, soft and light as a lullaby. Something about trees and flowers and the forests of home.

"We're gutting our own House." The girl throws the remote at the couch, then glares like she wants to throw me, too. "And all you can talk about is being frickin' dosed."

As opposed to gutting an indie with no military, no backup, and a whole population with nowhere to go? I almost shoot back.

Except she's right.

The knife burns in my hand. I wave at the screen. "How can they gut anyone? We have no ruler. Don't they have to find the Heir first, to sign off on that?"

Only a House Lord would have authority enough to make that kind of call.

"Lady Galton insisted," says the girl. "She thinks the other two Houses will launch an attack. Apparently they're allied now and hate our guts, and wars require fuel."

"The other Houses are allied?" I ask. "Since when?"

"Since one of Lord Fane's kids married the Westlet Heir. The Lady's got everyone so freaked, even the Prime didn't argue."

Of course he wouldn't. A new fuel supply would serve him, too.

I return the knife to its drawer. "What do you want?"

The girl throws a thumb at the screen. "This on the feeds, like your mother does her thing. People need to see this, they need to know."

"And she can hack the core-splitters," the skinny kid says. "She blew the Archive and planted a virus in the core House network. She can hack anything."

"A virus?" The feeds hadn't mentioned a virus.

The kid closes his eyes as if watching the code dance. "It's beautiful. They can't stop it, not even the best of them.

They search and search and just when they think they understand, it becomes something else. Your mother is a god."

That's where they're getting the god thing from? Something Mom did to the network? A virus that's still spreading?

I look to the girl.

She crosses her arms. "Where is Millie Oen?"

And here we go. Again.

"Mom's dead." I push the drawer closed, hard.

It doesn't drown out the girl's snort. "She wouldn't be caught in her own explosion."

"Well, she was."

"How do you know?"

"I just *do*, all right?" I feel it. The same way I felt Yonni—no recourse, no hope, no way to explain except that it just *is*.

The girl crosses the room and leans over the counter island that separates us, fingers tight on the ledge. "We lost one of our best people to Enactors over you—"

"Me? How's that my—"

"And our home is slated for scrap. 'I just do' won't cut it. If we go down, I'm taking you with us. You think the Archive explosion was bad? Just you wait."

I almost tug the knife out again. "And what am I supposed to do? Bring her back to life?"

She doesn't flinch, she doesn't even seem to breathe. "Figure. It. Out."

The skinny kid steps closer, too. "There's a control point. That's how she's playing messages out and killing the power. There's a datahost trigger somewhere, and you know where it is."

"Do I?" I snap.

He nods with regal assurance. Hell, he could double for Mrs. Divs.

The girl pulls a small digisheet from her pocket and slaps it on the counter. "We've made five vids—space them out, bunch them up, put them on a goddamn loop—I don't care. Just get them on the feeds. Otherwise, I swear I will hunt down and eviscerate every person in your life you remotely give a shit about, starting with that pretty boy two floors down."

My eyes snap to hers.

"Or maybe dear old dad, currently shacked up on level four." She grins, and my lungs give out.

The skinny kid slides up behind her. His smile fresh, devastating and real.

"Don't worry." He reaches across the counter to touch my forehead with soft fingers, like a benediction. "It's okay. You'll save us. You can be a god, too."

I POUND ON NILES'S DOOR WITH THE SIDE OF MY FIST. "You in there? You better be in there."

No answer. The door a blank, the hall a blank, and Niles a potential blank, too—lying dosed and unconscious on the goddamn floor.

My fault. No one would register his existence if not for me. Kissing him in the damn street—the whole House probably saw. If the Brinkers know, it's a sure bet the Enactors do. They'll think I've given him all of Mom's secrets—which, guess what? I may actually have.

Thanks, Mom. Hope you're enjoying hell.

I pound harder. Another second and I'll kick my way in. "*Niles.*"

The door opens and there he is—hair mushed, shirt askew, lashes blinking. He rubs them with the back of one hand, while reaching for me with the other. "Kit? What's wrong?"

Sleeping? How the hell could he be sleeping?

Probably because he got none last night.

I grab his collar, pull it aside, and check the base of his neck. Make a full circuit, feeling for punctures. Nothing.

They haven't got to him yet.

"Kit?" Much more awake now.

I come round to face him. "How do you feel? Was anyone here?"

"No," he drags out the word. "Why?"

I press two fingers under his jaw and check for a pulse—as if he isn't standing right here. I snatch my hand back.

Pull it together, Kit. Threats don't work if you kill the person first.

Except the Brinker wasn't making threats. Those were promises.

I need to check on Dad.

"Sorry, sorry." I skip back and toward the elevator. "Didn't mean to wake you. Go back to sleep."

"Oh hell no." Niles sprints ahead to block the way, hands on hips. "You can't give me a heart attack and then just take off."

"Doesn't seem to have done much damage."

I sidestep and he moves with me, bouncing on his toes. "I love how you think I'm not serious," he says.

"I love how you think I care," I snap.

His heels hit the floor, his eyes narrowed. "What's going on?"

"Nothing."

"Bullshit. It's been, what? A half hour? What the hell happened in—" He stops, hand pressing the back of his neck. "The Brinkers?"

Lord, he's smart. No one should be that smart.

"No, of course not." I inch back. He follows. "Why would

you think that?" My back hits wood. His hand flattens on the wall beside my head.

"They threaten you?" His mouth flatlines with his eyebrows, both drained of light. "Where are they?"

"Nowhere. There were no Brinkers."

He's close enough to kiss, whole body leaning in. "Did anyone ever tell you that you're a really shitty liar?"

I swallow. "Once or twice."

"What did the Brinkers want?"

"Not a damn thing."

"Kit." Dark. The kind of dark that'd go on the hunt for scary people, who would then land him dead in a ditch.

"Niles." Dark and just as edged. He has to give this up. "You're scaring me."

That pulls him back, a full three paces as his fingers press to his nose, then run through his hair. "When did they grab you?"

"It's *fine*. I'm fine, you're fine, we're all fine. Let it go, okay?"

"Nothing about this is fine!"

"Well, yelling about it won't make it better."

"I'm not yelling!" The words bounce off the ceiling, echo down the hall.

We stare at each other.

He scrubs his face. "Fine. I'm an asshole. A loud asshole."

"You're not an asshole."

He looks ready to kick something. "Did they hurt you?"

"No, I told you. They weren't even here."

"Kit—"

I hold up my hand and he stops, hands knots at his sides. I move to the stairwell.

"You can't just—"

But I'm gone.

THE LAST ADDRESS I HAVE FOR DEE LANDS ME IN THE heart of East 5th, between a skeletal flightwing dock and a shoptower of greasy takeout and hot sex. There's a sign.

Dee's tower sags in broken balconies and busted windows. No security or intercoms. I walk right into the lobby without a pass. Multilegged things skitter across the patchwork floor and up gray walls that might have had patterns once. Maybe still do, under the dirt.

Last I knew Dee had hooked up with some high-end dealer, who'd set her up with her own suite. It was all she could talk about, how Yonni's place couldn't compare.

She couldn't have meant here.

If Yonni saw this, she wouldn't have banned Dee from her suite—even after Greg's fiasco with Missa's meds.

Or maybe not. Maybe Yonni would have considered it justice.

The elevator doesn't work. The narrow stairwell winds under spitting lights and empties into a de-carpeted hall. The carpet lies rolled in a corner. Door 210 sits under one of three busted lights, absorbing the dark between black wood and gray handles. I knock, soft knuckled.

No one answers.

Skip this. I should just turn around and go.

Except, without my transaction card, I won't make any headway with Decker.

I need that bracelet.

I knock harder. "Dee, it's Kit."

Low swears filter through, followed by muffled thuds.

"I'm not joking, Dee," I say. "Open the door or I'll pop it."

And considering I got that particular skill from her son, she knows I'll make good. The door opens like magic.

Dee, pink-nailed, fluffy-haired, and grinning like she's happy to see me.

So Greg's here, then.

"Kit!" Bright and cheery, all Lady of the Tower. "What a happy surprise!"

"I bet." I push past her. The suite's even worse than the hall. Apparently, there was a reason for pulling the carpet. What's left in here is black and crunches with my steps. So would the walls if I touched them. They're crusted.

I bite my cheek.

Don't get sidetracked, Kit. Not now.

"Come on out, Greg," I tell the only other door in the place. Probably to the bathroom. Not a bedroom, because the bed sits next to the kitchen. If a rolling cart, a sink, and a fridge count as a kitchen.

Dee folds her arms. "Greg isn't here."

I cross the room and open the lone door. Greg tumbles to the carpet, hands and knees buried in whatever is growing on the floor.

"Dammit, Kit!" He scrambles, and my gut blackens with his fingers. He wipes his hands on his shirt—a new, crisp shirt that hasn't spent the last week glued to his frame.

I'm going to be sick.

"I didn't know what to do, okay?" he says, palms out, and I swear some of the dirt slithers. "Gerry's kicking me out of the boarding tower and those kids swore they just wanted to talk to you. It wasn't supposed to be a big deal."

"You dosed me, Greg."

"And obviously, you're fine." Dee jacks a cigarette pack from her back pocket and bounces one out with shaking fingers. "He's trying to stay out of Feverfed."

"The moon lockup?" I ask. Not even our planet's moon, but the third one over. The worst of the lot. The one people don't come back from. "How the hell did you get slated for that?"

"You saying you care?" Greg shakes, too, eye whites tinted yellow. He drops the cigarette his mother offers. It sinks into the carpet. He retrieves it, doesn't notice the smudged dark coating its end. I snatch the cig before he puts it in his mouth.

He swears. "Really, Kit? I can't even get a smoke?"

"Do you *want* to die?" I crush the cig to powder, drop what's left on the floor. Then step close and jam my hand into his right back pocket—where he always kept his money as a kid.

Some things don't change.

He jumps. "What the—?"

I pull away, my now-sticky transaction card held high. His cheeks burn with something like shame.

There's doping your cousin, and then there's robbing her unconscious form. Of course, he also stole pain meds from the love of his grandmother's life, so maybe nothing was ever sacred to him.

"Sorry," he says.

"No." Dee starts forward, trips on a half-eaten chair. "You do not apologize to *her*."

Of course not. I am the heartless daughter of a mass-murdering god.

I turn around and walk out.

THIRTY-TWO.

I stand at the cross street four blocks from Dee's and ask the transaction card to repeat the balance. The big red digits don't change.

0 3 2.

In the space of a day, Greg managed to burn through whatever the Brinkers paid him and my three hundred reds.

Sorry, two hundred sixty-eight.

Drugs? A second debt to Decker?

I can't bargain with this. I'll have to steal the bracelet back. And figure out how the hell it works before Decker tracks me down.

And he will. Nobody crosses Decker.

DECKER'S ALLEY GROWLS IN THE DEEPENED LIGHT
and chomps its graffiti teeth. His impassive door barricaded from the inside out. A lost cause even with my popping skills. What little they are.

But like Mom says, there's more than one way to rewrite the grid.

I look up. Past the teeth and the stone walls, the busted lights and the barred windows, to the half-chewed roofline eight stories above. For a tower, it barely warrants the name.

And along all eight of those stories clings an escape lift. A skinny ladder that turns into a skeletal stairwell around level four or five. Rusted and splitting from the wall in places, but workable. I've seen worse.

A subeight-story fall probably wouldn't kill me. If it does, well, my deal with Niles ended last night.

I climb.

The rungs flake hot. Stick to my palms and crawl under my nails. My shoes scrape and the ladder creaks—if Decker's here, I'm screwed—but the metal holds. And Decker shouldn't be here. He has a schedule, and I knew it by heart when I was trying to track down meds for Yonni.

I zoom up the first story and a half, slow into the third. My arms burn by the time I hit the stairwell, but then my legs take over and it's smooth flying. The escape lift returns to ladder form for the last story, and I haul myself onto the roof. Stand on the ledge and survey my conquered mountain. Or rather, the alley and the flat stone wall of the tower across the way.

I am a roof-climbing god.

Something skitters in the edge of my vision. Or someone. I jump backward onto the rooftop and drop behind the ledge. Wait a beat and peek over. Lots of painted teeth and grime. No people.

None visible. Probably a bird. It was totally a bird.

Right.

Life loves to kick you when you're high, Yonni used to say. *And low. And whenever the hell else it feels like.*

Missa had been at breakfast that morning, the only one of Yonni's entourage ever allowed to stay overnight even before Missa gave us the suite. I liked Missa better at breakfast. She looked like a messy old lady with oily hair and pale pink lips. At dinner Missa looked exactly like what she was—a picture-perfect lordling who could buy, sell, and fillet us with the flick of a finger.

But at breakfast Missa's skin had spots and lines. She'd leaned in and whispered loud enough for Yonni to hear, *And when it does, you run to the people who love you, because even life can't kick that.*

Don't you go filling my girl's head with bullshit, Yonni had snapped from the kitchen. But she smiled, too. That sly, subtle twist she backed by warm eyes and a heart that never faded.

Not until Missa died.

I twist onto my back and lay. Just lay. Sky a golden ring of towers and smog. A tiny, tight, impossible band that shrinks until it rips my chest in two.

"And what if there isn't anybody?" I ask the small, cragged sky. "What if there's no one left?"

Then go out and find more someones, says Yonni, except, no—that sounds more like Missa. Yonni would say something like, *then be the one someone else runs to.*

Or maybe they wouldn't say anything, and I'm just lying on my back on a dealer's rooftop in East 5th having conversations with the dead.

Because that's how I roll.

I peek over the ledge. The alley's clear, so whatever I thought I saw either didn't exist or plans to ambush me. Guess there's only one way to know.

I stand, brush myself off, and head across the empty roof to the stairwell door. It opens without hassle.

So far, so good.

The stairs are dark and I'm quiet going down. Round and round the stuffy concrete box, hand light on the support rail.

The door at the bottom opens easily. Quiet, but not silent. I hold my breath in the patchy dark.

Nothing. No answering sound.

Okay, maybe too good.

I creep down the hall, right along the edge. The peeling wall scrapes my shoulder, even burns, but there's no helping that. The central strip creaks. Ceiling lights spit as I pass under, spotlight my progress. Hopefully Decker doesn't have cameras.

He probably has cameras.

Just find the bracelet, I tell myself. *Then run like hell.*

The Brink kids will probably get to me first. Decker will have to wait his turn.

The hall ends in the final door. It's cracked, just a sliver. Not locked and barricaded but silent and beckoning.

Much too good.

Decker knows I'm here.

Run, scream the hairs on the back of my neck. *Why aren't you running yet?*

Because everyone I know doesn't deserve to be hunted down by the damn Brinkers. Especially not Niles. He didn't sign up for that. Nobody signed up for that. Not Dee, in her damn hovel. Not Dad or his latest. Not even Greg.

And they would be hunted. Vengeance is like that.

At least Yonni's well out of it. Death has its upsides.

I slide my fingers through the door handle and grip it tight.

"'I don't believe that fate falls on us no matter how we act,'" I say under my breath. Gilken steadies best when said aloud. "'But I do believe in a fate that falls on us unless we act.'"

So we act.

If it's a game, let's play.

I press the door hard enough that it bounces back off the wall. Stride into the black pitch. "Hey, Decker."

"See?" A high purr just behind my ear as the door clicks shut. "This is why I like you."

I jump, spin away from his scraping voice. Lightning skids from my neck to twist with my shoulder. Not quite a knife, not quite a needle, but hot and spitting.

I flail, hands tangled with the dark and an endless collection of things—smooth, grated, sharp, rough—a sliding racket, ricocheting junk.

Decker swears. I crash to my knees amid the junk piles, burning up and dizzy as hell. Skin crawling away from where his blade hit. It fizzes.

Not again. No goddamn asshole is dosing me *again*.

My fists hit the floor, and I focus every fiber on keeping the fire out of my brain before it shuts me down.

Awake. I will stay awake.

Light flares. Yellow refracting stars bounce off a thousand tumbled surfaces to cluster behind my eyes.

"You shouldn't have done that," says Decker.

I look over my shoulder—*on your feet, Kit, grab something heavy*—and see him, kneeling, his green shirt patterned red. He holds the shattered pieces of something painted and pretty. Splintered glass and gold trim halo his feet. He pets each shard. "You really shouldn't have done that."

"Put it on the tab," I think. Say?

Decker's eyes snap to mine with the force of a spark-bomb.

Shit.

He lunges.

I grab the steel lamp near my elbow and swing. Smash his head as he rams my chest. We fall. His slimy body dead weight. Ribs and chin and knees. I kick him off, heels skidding as I scramble through the endless junk. His collected treasures. My shoulder collides with something sharp, and the world upends in clatter—trinkets and tools flooding the gap between me and him.

Decker doesn't flinch. He doesn't even move.

"No." I crawl close, reach his side and turn him over. "I did not just kill you, you asshole. You are *not* dead."

His temple oozes, hair matted. There are red dots on the floor.

I freeze.

No, I *move*. Place two fingers to his neck and search. Nothing, more nothing.

A line of blood runs the gully of his nose, crests his upper lip.

"Artery's on the other side," I say aloud. Calm, even cold. My fingers are cold, skinny ice packs against his skinny neck. "Come on. Where are you? Where *are* you?"

A beat. Rhythm under my fingertips, strong and hot.

I sit back on my heels, hand sliding to the floor. Bone-less. Relief and beauty, my whole body an open world in a massive sky.

Alive. He has all his hopes and tomorrows. I didn't steal them.

I just busted half his shit.

The room spins as I haul myself up. Another table crashes, but I manage not to fall.

The bracelet. Get the bracelet and get out.

I weave my way to the big counter in the room's center. Peer through the smudged glass. So much glitter. Strings and pendants, rings and customized digicom earpieces. They sparkle.

My head sparkles. My shoulders and neck. Bright hot flairs.

"Bracelet," I chant, under my breath. "Bracelet, bracelet."

I move behind the counter, bust the lock, and open its

sliding back wide. Dig through the shallow boxes, cushioned displays, and hanging racks. I sort and pull. Check and recheck. Scan the same three shelves three times.

It's not here. Not Mom's bracelet, not Yonni's pendant. Which makes no sense, because this is where all the pricey stuff is kept.

All the stuff that's on display.

Shit.

The room stretches, vast and frantic. The bracelet could be anywhere. It could be somewhere else entirely. A back office? His private collection?

Another customer's pocket.

The floor sways. I brace my hands against the counter, arms straight and legs locked.

"No, you don't," I say. "You don't pass out. You go over, wake him up, and ask."

Because that worked so well last time.

My arms shake. They're heavy. Everything's heavy. My head weighs as much as a planet and wants to rotate more.

I'm going to fall over.

Not until I reach Decker, I won't. He's not that far. Just the other side of the House. Room. Whatever.

I round the counter and walk in a semistraight line. Manage not to step on anything. Not even Decker, spread-eagled and bloody.

He has a pulse. I checked. I remember checking.

I check again.

Somewhere down the hall a door scrapes, swooshes, and slams.

"Decker!" Deep, unknown, and male. "Where the hell are you, man? We were supposed to meet an hour ago."

My heart jumps through my throat and out my ears.

I move, trinkets scattering with my sliding feet.

Loud, too loud, there's nowhere to step that isn't loud.

"Decker?"

I hit the wall by the door and slam the lights off just as the door opens.

A man steps in, biceps inches from my nose. He has big, massive, both-my-hands-together-couldn't-wrap-around-them arms. I only come up to his shoulder.

I really am going to be sick.

He steps past me into the dark. "God dammit—stop with the games, Dec. I know you're here." His forearm rises and he half turns, reaching for me, the wall, the light.

I bolt.

"What the—?"

My legs are heavy, but my feet don't care. I burn through the hall, pass door after door. Footsteps behind, harsh and gaining.

I hit the exit with my forearms. The long, horizontal

handle flattening as I spill into the alley. I nearly slam into the wall opposite, elbow scraping stone as I skid a turn.

Fingers claw my back but slide off after a beat or three. A harsh grunt, a thud—maybe him hitting a wall. I don't know, I don't turn.

I run.

I COLLAPSE AGAINST THE WALL. A WALL. SOMEWHERE.

I don't know where. I don't know—

Stop, think.

I ran maybe four blocks, all toward home.

"East 5th." My chest heaves air too hot to swallow. "I'm in East 5th."

With no bracelet, few reds, and a highly pissed Decker—who now has motivation enough to get me before the Brinkers do.

I'll have to go back.

I press my forehead into the ridged stone, hands flat on either side. My toes are numb. And my elbows, which is weird. I shouldn't be awake right now, my whole body's an exclamation to that point.

I can't fight off a muscle man like this. Or Decker, who's probably awake by now.

Which means he can tell me about the bracelet.

Without the bracelet, we're all screwed.

I turn back. Push myself along the walkway, my sweaty hand streaking the windows of darkened storefronts.

"Kit?"

I spin and collapse into the glass.

Niles stands across the street, mouth open and staring. He's still in his rumpled button-up, though he seems a bit more together. Must be the smoothed hair.

He jogs across the empty street. "God, I've been looking everywhere! Where the hell did you—*Kit*."

Then he's here, at my shoulder. A magically materialized being.

"You're bleeding!" he says.

I lean into his chest and don't say a word.

"Kit? *Kit*." He pushes my hair off my shoulder, too busy checking my neck to hug me back.

Or kiss me. A kiss would be nice.

Niles raises his fingers. They're bloody. Some of the blood is more blue than red. He sniffs them. Tastes one.

"Ew," I say.

He stares like it's the most incredible thing he's ever heard. Or the most frightening. Incredibly frightening?

"How are you even standing right now?" he asks.

"Feet, toes, legs, bones."

And all of them have places to be.

I bypass him, whole body sliding along the window. He fills the space ahead, so we're leaning on the window together, and holds up his smeared hand. "This is avirimal."

The one dosing agent even Greg wouldn't deal in.

Well . . . shit.

"You don't know that," I say. "How can you know that?"

"It tastes like makieberris," he says.

"Wait—you know what avirimal tastes like?"

"My dad told me."

And his dad was into "appropriation." Hell, he probably appropriated doses. Very dose appropriate.

I giggle.

Niles rubs my arms. "Can you feel your elbows?"

"Why would I want to?"

He snorts, grin flashing out before he bites it back. "God, only you. Can you walk?"

"Of course I can walk." I shake him off. "Go home."

"Home? Home? I find you in East 5th—"

"One district over."

"Dosed to hell—"

"I'm awake, aren't I?"

"And bleeding."

"Ran into a door."

"And you want me to go home?"

"Our deal's off, right? Since yesterday? You don't have to keep me alive anymore."

Niles closes his eyes, goes so still he outclasses the shadows. Then he steps in, arms sliding loose around my waist as his forehead rests against mine. My whole body relaxes without checking first with my brain.

"The deal's still on." He sounds exhausted and a little worn. "Tell me what happened."

I fist my hands against his shirt to push him away. And

I will, I have to, it's just . . . he makes everything else intangible. Harder to hold, to care about. At least with his breath on my lips and his palms low on my back. "We need to have a fight or something, so they think you're not important."

He pulls back to see my face, so I let him see the truth of it.

"I'm going to get you killed," I say.

His expression blanks out, an empty wall-screen with no emotion. Even his voice doesn't comment. "Me? They threatened you with me?"

"Everyone. Anyone. You're in my general radius—look." I flatten my hand to his chest and work up the will to push. "Go home. I have stuff to do."

"You think those Brink kids can take me?" He tries for a smile, but even its angles are flat.

"'They crave life like water and drink death like wine,'" I say. Gilken understood courage. "They have everything to lose, and with that gone nothing to stop them."

"I don't understand."

"Their home world—Lady Galton's going to gut it. I've seen the core-splitters. Their planet will die and nothing will matter. Don't you see? Nothing will matter to them anymore. They'll kill everyone to get back at me, they'll—"

His kiss snatches the words off my tongue and swallows them whole.

"Please," I whisper. "Just go. I don't want you dead."

"I won't be," he says against my lips, a kiss in itself. "Whose son do you think I am?"

"But—"

Except he steals that word, too, and the seconds after. Whole minutes. Maybe my soul.

"Even if your mom blew ten Archives," he says into our breathy silence, "she couldn't touch my dad."

Holy hell.

"You're . . . not serious," I say.

He squeezes tighter, as if I'm the one stabilizing him. "Just tell me what the hell is going on."

So I close my eyes and do.

MOM ACTS AS MY PILLOWS. MY HEAD IN HER LAP AS I kneel on the cold clinic floor, Yonni's bed high and tubed to our right. Mom smooths my hair. I taste blood. Mine, I think. She rubs red between her fingertips. "Oh, brightheart, what did you get into?"

"I don't want to talk about it." I need to get up, scoot away. Except under her hand, my forehead hurts less.

"You haven't that option. We've reached the third and are nearing the fourth. Besides, the elevator's stopped on your floor."

I sit up, palms scraping the cold tile. I see the bed, the empty sterile walls, but I can also see the elevator. Duel images my brain takes in stride.

The lift doors open and men pour out.

Mom watches them, too. Her dress shimmers like the city haze as she sniffs her red fingers. A little sweet, a little burnt.

Everything clicks.

"Scent maps," I say. "You're mapping me. Planting suggestions in my brain."

She smiles and traces my cheek. "Good girl. I pressed a receptor patch to your arm when you came to visit me. Fast dissolving and untraceable, but brief. It'll last two weeks, then I'll fade out."

She put something on me? In me?

Of course she did.

I wait for the anger to kick in. It'd be so much easier to be angry. "But you're already dead."

I know she's dead. Know it so deep it weaves through my blood.

"Yes," she says. "It was necessary."

The men march down the hall now, five total, and Dee's with them.

"Then how is this happening?"

She scrunches her nose at me. "You're a smart girl, it's not hard. Ask the right questions. It's a matter of heart."

One of the men pounds the door.

I sit bolt upright on the couch—my couch—the pounding not just in my head but my ears. A sheet slips off my legs to puddle in the sun spots from the windows. Bright sun, pre-afternoon but well into morning. The air's thick, almost metallic.

"Kit Franks." A door-splitting knock. "This is the Records Office. If you refuse us entry, then under the authority of Record 269A–495, we will enter unaided."

Wait, they're real?

I sniff the air, taste the burned and the sweet.

Mom mapped me. She planted a patch and *mapped* me.

Pound pound pound.

"Coming, I'm coming!" I call.

I swing my feet to the floor, scrub my face. Can still feel

the echo of Mom's fingers. Now *that* wasn't real. I don't think. My shoulder burns up to my neck. I rub the ache and find gauze—a thin, neat strip.

Niles. Niles patched me up then said he'd be back.

The pounding worsens. Any more and they'll bust it in. "This is not a game, Miss Franks."

No shit.

"Okay, okay." I haul myself onto mostly steady legs and walk to the door. I barely get it open before a hand forces it wide. They barrel in, five men in dark blue suits with the dark purple and green cuffs of Recorders. Four large hoverdiscs bob along behind them—digiloaders certified to carry a street-hover's worth of weight—each stacked with folded boxes.

The men are all of a height and spread out on a mission, each marching into a different room.

My hands tighten at my sides. "What's going on?"

The only man without a digiloader at his heels steps forward. He looks just like the others. A little blonder maybe, broader-shouldered, but the same flat expression. Same dead eyes.

He'd happily rend me to ash and dance on my grave.

The man thrusts a thin digisheet contract under my nose, transparent except for the text. "Under Record 782-H of the Rights of Inheritance, upon death all possessions of the deceased will transfer to his or her eldest child."

"No, the suite's mine." I grab the sheet before it smashes my nose. "Yonni made a will; it's recorded."

And so far, no one's mentioned Dad.

"Yes," says a different voice. Dee's voice. "But the will only specifies the suite itself. It didn't mention the things in the suite."

She leans against my doorframe and looks . . . pretty. Hair smoothed into a professional bun, white blouse airy and feminine. Stark skirt and heels. No jangling bracelets, no blaring jacket or studs. She could be a lordling.

She could be Yonni.

All around, the Recorders flutter. Open boxes and fill them. A suited storm of feet and hands.

But here, it's quiet. Calm.

"You're stealing my stuff." I sound almost disinterested.

"No, *my* stuff." She flicks the digisheet from my hand and highlights a passage with a smooth swipe. "You're lucky I don't press charges, keeping me from my inheritance for so long."

The text agrees. Perfect legal sentences, tidy and above board. How did I not know this? How did Dee not know this? She fought like hell when the will was read, but all of that discussion hinged on the suite. We never talked much about things, especially since I gave Dee most everything she wanted.

She never cared about Yonni's stuff, except for resale value. There's nothing left worth selling.

But then, this isn't about Yonni.

I search Dee's face for something to hate, wait for the anger to hit. It doesn't.

Two of the men brush by, carrying Yonni's bed. Even cracked, it's nicer than anything else in Dee's suite.

The lead Recorder waits, itching for a scene. Begging for it. He'd love to take down Millie Oen's daughter on a technicality. Who wouldn't? Dee sees it, too, and her eyes hold the dare. *Go ahead, cause a scene. Be that stupid.*

But I'm not into hopeless battles. Most survivors aren't, as a rule.

I hand the digisheet back. "That must have taken some digging."

She leans close with wide burgundy lips. "You touch my son again, and you'll lose more than this."

"He's the one who dosed me, remember?"

"And he's facing Feverfed," she whispers in my ear. "What have you ever faced?"

"Today?" I bite. "You."

She grins, the mirror image of Yonni. "And don't you forget it."

THE RECORDERS TAKE EVERYTHING. FURNITURE, dishes, curtains. My clothes, my shoes. If it's not nailed down or on my person, if I can't prove I bought it with my own money, it's gone.

Dee knows how to make a point.

Yonni's favorite heels with the blue spikes. The box of patterned fabric for the quilt she promised to make some-day. Her kitschy cat figurines with the purple skin and big eyes. Even my Gilken quotepad from the fridge—all boxed up and hauled out.

I follow the Recorders with their digiloaders down to the tower lobby. Stand, arms folded, atop the outer steps as they load boxes in a hauler-bus too big for the occasion.

Dee preens. Blows me a kiss as the hauler's rear door slams. Smiles at the Recorder who opens the smaller door of a high-end streethover. The rest of the group splits between the hauler and hover, loads up and ships out. The engines purr down the street. Turn a corner four blocks down, and disappear.

Everything Yonni was, everything she loved, everything that mattered—is gone. All gone.

I didn't fight. I didn't kick or scream or stop them. I let Dee walk into Yonni's place, which I promised to never do, and walk out with the whole of Yonni's life—which Yonni also would have extracted a promise for, if she'd had any idea that'd be on the table.

The street's empty, the engines' whirring long since gone. The sun's high, harsh and blinding.

I don't move, have nowhere to go. The suite's empty. I'm empty.

Behind me, the lobby door opens and closes. A withered hand finds my arm.

"It wasn't me," Mrs. Divs says. "I didn't tell anyone about your dad."

"I know." It cracks, stuck to my tongue.

Her hand rubs up and down, back and forth. "Come on in, now. The heat's gettin' worse."

My legs are locked, feet rooted. Here, on the steps, I'm calm, firm, and collected.

I don't know what will happen if I move. If the calmness will stick.

Mrs. Divs tugs. "You can't stay out here forever."

Really? Watch me.

"Kit." She imbues my name with power, like a charm. "We've lost much worse than this. You come on inside."

Yonni. She means Yonni.

My heels shift and move. I don't fall over or melt into screams. I don't lose any composure at all.

Apparently, I'm fine.

Go me.

Mrs. Divs props the door with her hip and I push it open farther so she can step through. The entryway is unnaturally quiet, post the Recorders' determined tread. No inquisitive neighbors stick their heads out. I guess the potential trouble isn't worth the curiosity. Only Mrs. Divs's door hangs open, her thumping cane setting our pace.

"Can I have a cookie?" I ask. If I close my eyes I can smell them, even out here in the hall. Except, in my head the cookie jar sits on a table outside a pastry shop, amid a garden of green. And it isn't even a jar, but a fat sticky roll piled with enough frosting to put me in a coma.

I could use a coma.

"Have you had breakfast?" Mrs. Divs asks.

Well, that answers that question.

"Never mind," I say.

Niles plied me with a sandwich last night after bringing me home, so it's not like I need the food.

Mrs. Divs pats my arm. "You eat breakfast, we'll talk."

We reach her suite. Her wall-screen runs unmuted today, voices filtering through the cracked door. Or rather, a voice.

Mom's.

I throw the door wide and skid to a stop before the screen.

Mom wears the same airy purple blouse as before,

hair swept in a knot. Her eyes are half-closed, lips moving through a lullaby. Reciting verses that, long ago, she used to sing.

"You see us broken? We'll see you dead. A mask behind where stars aligned and ate regret."

She sways with the cadence, hinting at melody. Notes just under the surface, trapped, unheard.

I let them out, sing them in a whisper to accompany her words.

"You see us broken? We'll watch you fall. A kiss away from the trick that played us all for false."

Mom closes her eyes like she can hear.

Or maybe she's remembering how Dad used to ball her out about it. *You know that's a shitty song to sing to a kid, right?*

But Mom only shook her head. *It's her heritage,* she'd say and sing it anyway. So I would, too.

Like I am, now.

And like then, I'm singing in tandem—and not just with Mom.

"Close your eyes against the blood," joins Mrs. Divs. "Promise yourself it was all for love."

"And understand ours for you." Mom raises a thin silver remote with a single button and doesn't quite smile.

"Account closed," she says and presses down.

The wall-screen blinks out and sparks at the corners. The suite lights flick on, burn white, then pop. A battery of pops that end in absence. Chained echoes bolting from fixture to socket, living room to kitchen.

Entryway to street.

I run to the lobby and bang through the outer door. All down the thoroughfare, streetlights hiss and spit despite being dark. The tower across the way burns bright from a hundred windows and blacks out. The one beside it follows suit, then the one behind that. On and on. An orchestrated light circus, with movements and beats and synchronicity.

And once the blast hits, light disappears.

Thirty seconds, less, and our whole block's down. Everything's down that I can see from street level.

The roof. I could see more from the roof.

I swing back my tower's door. Through the glass Mrs. Divs stands in the entryway, just outside her suite. Both hands clasped on the cane firmly set in front of her, back straighter than I've ever seen.

She meets my eyes. Hers aren't terrified, or even shocked. And I can hear her soft voice singing with mine.

The lullaby. Mom's lullaby. The words, the tune. She knew them. The song of the Accountants, the song of the indies.

Mrs. Divs knew.

She raises the head of her cane first to her mouth, and then her temple in a simple salute. Not a Galton salute, but one I've only ever seen in Mom's late-night meetings with her "special" friends.

What. The. *Hell.*

"For a moment there," Mrs. Divs calls, muffled through the glass, "I was afraid she'd allow you to undo us, but I see she hasn't forgotten who she is. If you see your mother, give her my blessing and apologize for my doubt."

Then Mrs. Divs turns on impossibly steady heels and slips into her suite.

She's an Accountant. God, she's—she's like Mom. She *knew.*

I yank the lobby door, but it swung shut behind me and won't budge. I pull my keypass from my pocket—that I still have on me, thank God—and press it to the security lock.

Nothing happens. Its embedded screen dark and burnt, hot brown at the edges. I try again.

Which would absolutely work, because, of course, my run-down tower's security system would somehow survive a block-wide—maybe even city-wide—blackout.

Shit.

I pound the door. "What the hell is going on?"

Mrs. Divs doesn't answer or doesn't care, her door shut tight.

"I know you can hear me," I yell. "Don't act like you can't."

"Kit Franks?" says a deep voice at my back.

I yip and spin.

Two men stand on the steps below, both around Dad's age, with authoritative menace blazoned all over them. Enactors for sure, or higher-end thugs.

That was fast. The power's gone, so, of course, it has to do with me.

Hell, it probably does.

Screw that.

I don't think, I swing. Catch one smack on the chin—jutting square and hard as stone. My fingers scream, bones creaking.

Or maybe his bones. Lord, I hope so.

They move in a blur, suited arms and dark hair. Grab my fist and twist it behind me. Push me to my knees. The flash of a dosing tube, a sting at my neck.

"Seriously?" I say. "You've got to be—"

ECHO

WAKE UP. IT'S TIME, COME ON."

A quick pain high in my arm, breath on my cheek. I'm lying somewhere . . . hard? My head throbs. It's dark. When I open my eyes, it's still dark. Everything is dark.

What. The. Hell.

"That's it. Can you sit?"

"Niles?" I ask. It's his voice. His palm under my shoulder, helping me rise.

"Look at me. I need to check your pupils."

I blink. It's him, the outline of him. Cheeks pale in the dimness, hair shadowed and lost. Fingertips spreading my eyelid apart as he peers in, face close enough to kiss. So I do. Taste the wear of the day and the humid dark, the warmth that sears his very skin. He burns with it, a desperate hum of tension and wire that curls my ribs and pulls even as he pulls away, anchoring us apart with a palm to my cheek. His thumb skims my lips where his just were, soft as air.

"You're here," I say.

"Yeah."

My words soft, his cracked.

My head's heavy but not cloudy, muscles sore without screaming. I don't feel good, but not so bad, either. My neck hurts the most. I rub the assorted holes and scratches. I've got quite the collection. "Who dosed me this time?"

He laughs. A breathy, silent, mirthless thing that wanes as he stares into the dark. "I found the bracelet."

"What?" I search his face, but even this close it's hard to see. "Wait, how—"

"Decker."

Oh shit.

"What the hell were you thinking?" I push closer, feel for wounds. "You went alone? Did you get caught? I know Decker doesn't look like much, but—"

"I'm fine, Kit."

He doesn't sound fine. Or not fine, for that matter. His fingers dig holes in my skin.

I wince. "Ow."

"Shit, sorry." His hold evaporates and we separate. He stays close but doesn't touch. I hear him, though, the pull of his breath before he finds words. "The bracelet. There's nothing special about it."

Something's wrong.

I scan behind him, but it's just black. What light there is doesn't seem to come from anywhere. The air's stale, without breeze or exhaust fumes. Enclosed. If I yelled, it might echo.

We're alone in a hole in the dark.

If we are alone. I have my doubts.

I lean close, lips to his ear. "How bad are you hurt? Can you run?"

His cheek presses into mine a heartbeat, less. He doesn't whisper back. "I'm not hurt, Kit."

Not yet.

The Brinkers must have jumped him outside of Decker's. Or maybe this is Decker's doing.

"I told you to be careful, that they drink death like wine."

His forehead breaks into wrinkles. "What the hell does that even mean?"

"When you're clear, look it up."

And he will be clear. I'll make damn sure.

I stand in one swift motion, hand braced on his shoulder as the dizziness hits, and yell into the dark. "Niles doesn't know shit about the bracelet! He never even met Mom. Lord, he never met me until a few days back—and look how that's worked out for him."

Niles's tension could suspend cables. "Kit." Almost inaudible.

"You want to ask me something?" I call. "You ask *me*. And you won't get shit for answers until he's clear."

"In that case," says another voice entirely.

A harsh finger snaps and light flares. Spotlights, not overheads. Blue-tinged, battery-powered backups aimed straight for my skull. I flinch, try to blink sanity back into my retinas.

We're in some kind of large room or hangar, walls sketchy beyond the spotlights.

A man steps into the blue glare, flanked by two others. Not the Brinkers with backup or even Decker with thugs, but a broad-shouldered, sleek-suited man. Tall and oozing power like grace.

The Prime.

The Head of the Enactors, the most powerful person in our House apart from the currently lost bloodling Heir and the wife of the late Lord, stands not six feet away and smiles.

Oh . . . shit.

My nails bite Niles's shoulder. He doesn't make a sound.

"You," I say.

His smile widens, and there's something oddly familiar about it. Resonant.

"Me," he says.

And not just him. The flanking Enactor on the right has the ghost-pale skin and glaring eyes of the power technician.

Well, I started this round.

"You want answers?" I ask. "Let Niles go."

The Prime regards me, eyebrows raised. I may have started, but he'll finish and we both know it.

He motions Niles up with two effortless fingers, and Niles matches with efficiency. Slipping from my grasp and on his feet almost before my hand registers the motion.

"May I introduce you to my son?" asks the Prime. "Or perhaps you've met."

What?

Niles stands at attention, stares not so much at me as past. Blue light threads his black hair and glistens along his shuttered eyes. The impenetrable blank of his cheeks and chin. He says nothing, looks like nothing—not smart or relentless or irritating. No hidden warmth that multiplies and melts my skin.

Niles? The Prime's son? But they look nothing alike. Their height, their facial structure, their eyes—the Prime's are too round and light and—

Amusement flicks through the Prime's gaze, slides into a small smile, and I see it. The Niles in him.

My dad excels at leverage, he'd said.

Think, Decker, he'd said.

"Appropriation," I say. My own smile crawls out of nowhere at the beauty of it. The perfection. A razor's edge he balanced while I fell. Am falling. My stomach a

247

sickened spiral that rips on every broken crag and doesn't land. Can't—there's no purchase. The only solid ground I had was him.

So, of course, he wasn't real.

I laugh with all the heat scraping my eyes and throat. "Appropriation. God. I can't say you don't play fair."

The statue of Niles becomes more statuesque. He makes a pretty statue. Cast him in marble to preside over the city's high gardens. Probably will, what with him being the son of the Prime. Hell, if an Heir never appears and the Prime and Lady Galton duke it out to establish a new bloodling line, Niles may wind up ruling the House.

I'd have kissed a House Lord.

I can still feel his lips. My heart's answering glow. Jack-knifed now, but . . . there.

Niles watches with his stone smooth face, and probably sees everything. My laughter dies.

"I wonder," says the Prime, "if you grasp the current state of affairs."

"I'm trapped in a room with the Prime and his—his son," I say. "Think I've got it."

The Prime moves closer—easy, graceful, he damn near controls the air. "This little rebellion? Your 'Accounting'? Won't last."

"My Accounting," I repeat.

"'*Close your eyes against the blood,*'" he recites, in Mom's same singsong. "'*Promise yourself it was all for love.*'"

He's heard it before. He knows.

"That's just a stupid lullaby," I say.

"Come now, aren't we past that?" He closes in, eats the space. "This power-out of yours won't last."

So the power's still down. No wonder they're running off of battery-backed spotlights. Mom must have blown the city's energy grid. Probably had it on a timer.

"Don't confuse me with Mom," I say. "You think I have brains enough to manage a power-out?"

"Doesn't take much to activate a trigger."

"What trigger? You have everything I had of Mom's."

And Dee has everything else, full stop.

"You mean this?" The Prime pulls Mom's bracelet from his jacket pocket, to dangle it aloft. The light catches it in starbursts. "Worthless."

Niles gave the Prime my mother's bracelet. He must have. Because there it is, in the Prime's hand—charms tinkling in a silver ribbon that clatters to the floor, chain curling in the paved dirt. Even there, it shines.

I stand still and straight and do not—do not—retrieve it.

"It has no hidden circuitry." The Prime shrugs in a Niles-like way. "And I don't need silver or glitter."

The real Niles might atrophy if he doesn't move soon.

His name probably isn't even Niles.

My stomach wants to eat my heart.

"Like I said," I repeat. "That was everything of Mom's I had."

"No, not everything." The Prime reaches one long finger and taps the center of my forehead. "You have this."

Mapping.

He's going to mind map me. Pry my brain for answers. Piece me apart.

Wonder how that works with a temporary scent map patch. Probably not well.

The Prime's finger trails over my temple, down my cheek, and under my chin. He lifts.

"Don't think I don't know what her digivirus is doing." Soft enough for a whisper. "Why she chose the Archive, the real project she set in motion. It was never about destroying the power grid, though I'm sure she felt it a nice perk." He leans near. Entirely too near. Another inch, and our noses would brush. "And don't think I won't stop her. This House is mine."

He's too close and too tall and twice my age at least, the bastard.

Yonni always said there was nothing worse than a man who flaunts power against those who have none.

"Really?" I say. "'Cause I thought the House was the

Heir's. Though if you're planning to usurp the line, good luck taking it from the Lady. I think she's got you beat."

He blinks. A slow blink. Lethal.

"Speculation," Niles says. He appears at my elbow, calm and disinterested. "Not the first time she's spouted random shit."

"Perhaps." The Prime leans away and takes his hand with him. I can still feel Niles's fingers. "We'll soon see."

"Shall I take her to the mapping center?" Niles asks.

The words shred all the bits of me still intact. There weren't many. I scan the space, but there's nowhere to run. Plus the flunkies in back have their dosers out.

"No, to holding," says the Prime. "We have to get the power on first."

"Hell no." I step away from their happy little family, nod at the silent Shadow/techie waiting in back. "You can send me with him."

The Prime's smile could gut a planet. "And what makes you think you have a say?"

THE STREETHOVER'S REAR DOORS HAVE NO INTERIOR handles. My seat has no cushion, a curved silver bench built into an enclosed pillbox that's empty but for me.

And Niles, beyond the partition window that separates my mobile prison from the hover's front seat. He steers us through the dead city. Skytowers loom in shadows, black-toothed gaps against the smoke-black sky. The haze saves the sky from being pitch, but not by much. There's no light to reflect.

The city is different. Haunted. No flashing ad-screens, no streetlights or bright shopfronts. Some of the cloudsuite towers glow blue in peppered windows, but even those are dim. We could almost be underwater, in one of the Outer Brink's black seas.

Seas that soon won't exist once the fuel extraction begins.

At least the Brinkers have nothing to hold over my head anymore. Niles is the Prime's son. They couldn't kill him if they tried.

And once word of my mapping hits their radar, Dee and Dad will be safe, too. There won't be enough left of me to make the Brinker's broadcast happen.

Niles catches my eye in the skinny mirror that reflects the street behind. I look away.

"The whole planet's down," he says, and the silence jumps. "There are riots in East 5th."

Not surprising.

I stare out the window.

"You were suicidal," says Niles.

My eyes snap to the mirror. He watches, hair soft in the interior's glow. Haloed.

"Holding" must be on the other side of the damn planet. We're going to wreck if Niles doesn't keep his eyes on the street.

"Wesfen said he had to break cover to keep you from jumping, which meant one less eye on you."

So the power technician has a name.

I return to the window.

"Most of Dad's people are tied up with the Heir search. I was bred for infiltration, and Dad thought you could use a personal touch." He sounds different now. There's culture to his cadence. It's nice. I hate it. "Especially after he brought up the mapping and you laughed at him. The damn *Prime*. Met his eyes and just . . ." Niles shakes his head. "That was the second time I saw you."

He can shut up anytime.

"Dad thinks you're the key to Oen's virus, so we had to keep you intact."

Yeah, and mapping won't screw with that at all.

Niles must read my brain. "The mapping is my fault. It's too risky and Dad wouldn't have used it, but I sold him on the bracelet—that you believed it was the key. And since it's not . . . we have to search your subconscious for answers."

So my being fried up as a slimy vegetable is on him, too. Fantastic.

I hope the Prime is right, that Mom has a project. A reason.

I hope the virus destroys them all.

The streethover slows. The darkened city gets darker, and we enter some kind of building. Warehouse maybe? Walls and ceiling swallowing the hover as its forward beams outline a world of pavement and dust.

We jerk to a stop, engine still humming as Niles turns in his seat. We face each other through the partition window.

"Aren't you going to chew me out?" he asks. "Haul my ass over the carpet? Don't you have anything to say?"

"To you?" Flat. Nothing.

I will be nothing, if they map me.

But the power's still out, the city still dark, and they haven't mapped me yet.

Niles closes his eyes, forehead thudding into the window. He doesn't seem to care.

If my door had a handle, I'd be gone. I search the dark for something to see.

"If you could do anything," Niles asks, softer now, "go anywhere, had no ties, what would you do?"

"Other than break your neck?"

He flinches, but nods.

I'd go home and raid Mrs. Divs's cookie jar.

Except that'd land me with a treacherous Accountant and singer of lullabies who locked me out. The cookies are probably poisoned.

I link my hands behind my head and stare into the hover's ceiling.

"I'd go eat pastries in Westlet," I say, "visit all their city bake shops, start my own travel show." I smile into his tight, wary face. "After I destroyed Galton, of course. Every last piece. I am my mother's daughter."

He doesn't move, doesn't seem to breathe. Dead eyes above his dead mouth. Then he opens his door, grabs a small bag, and slides it across the seat with him as he exits.

His door hangs open, the hover's engine still humming, as he opens mine.

Stupid.

As soon as my door cracks, I slam into it, sending him stumbling as I leap for the front seat. He grabs my wrist as I reach his door and hauls me into him, chest to chest. His free palm flattens on my back, the other reaching for my cheek. He kisses me, desperation made form. Blinding, even with my eyes closed. He is spark and fire, and I will burn him up. I grab the edge of his shirt, curl my fingers in his hair. His hands slide from my hips to neck to waist, until my whole body's a map of where he is and was and where I want him to be. He's a fuse, singed, busted, and cracking, and my eyes burn until they leak.

I feel it, the water, the trails. Taste the salt.

"Why you?" I ask under my breath, in my blood. "Dad I get, and Dee, and maybe even Greg, but you? Did this have to be a game? Did *you* have to—"

"It wasn't." His hot fingers find my cheeks. Smudge my tears between our skin. "Not in that way, not like you think."

It's too much. Whole worlds too much. He has no right to kiss me, and I have no damn sanity kissing him.

"Go to hell," I say.

He's as still as I am, but thrumming tension. It bleeds through his eyes and down his fingertips, which he pulls from my face. "Goodbye, Kit."

He swings into the streethover and has it in motion before his door slams. Rear orange lights burning streaks through the yawning door into the street. Disappear.

I'm alone.

All I'd have had to do was kick him, and I'd be half across the city by now. But no, I kissed him back.

That was probably the idea.

I gasp—laugh, sob?—hands cupped to my mouth. My ribs crack and I can't breathe. I can't—

"There's a limit," I whisper, or maybe just think—Gilken's words the only ones in my head that don't hurt. "'History records, but stories ground us. Prove that these limitless terrors have a limit, that our universe holds something greater than darkness and stronger than fear.'"

He was wrong. There's nothing here but fear and dark, the limits only on us—our souls—and nothing else. The terrors run rampant.

Though maybe not here. The Prime doesn't materialize in the offing, the Brinkers don't appear with a sparkblade to Dad's throat, and the one person more terrifying than them all just jumped into a hover and drove off.

Bastard.

My lungs calm, stop trying to eat themselves. I am quiet in a dark that may be greater than me but hasn't killed me yet.

Though not for lack of trying.

Except . . . it doesn't try. The shadows don't scamper. No Enactors sidle in to haul me away. Someone should have, by now.

I hold my breath, listening.

Nothing. No movement or sound.

If you could do anything, go anywhere, had no ties, what would you do?

Niles had grabbed a bag while getting out of the hover. His hands were empty when he left.

I crouch, fingers scanning the pavement. Rough stone, powdered dirt . . . stiff fabric, rounded and limp. A satchel? I find a flap, flip it over, and dig inside.

There's next to nothing. Some flat rectangles with round edges, a small box with hinges, and a fatter rectangle with buttons and rippled glass at one end.

A pocket light. I hit the button. Cool white blazes hot enough to blind. I bury it in the bag, and it glows through the fabric. I blink my eyes back to normalcy and ease the bag open.

A transaction card with 500 reds.

A pale ID card, its thin digitech screen looping through text. *Please scan print now, Jenna Flesk, setup not complete, please scan . . .*

A darker keypass with a miniature flightwing in the corner. I tap the emblem. Across the warehouse, blue running lights flair into the outline of a wing. Crest its smooth nose and flow into its tail. Black and small, and worth more than my suite and Mrs. Divs's inter-House communicator combined.

If you could do anything . . .

Oh, the *idiot*.

I dump the cards in my pocket, grab the bag, and almost throw it across the floor.

The Prime will know. Niles will show up empty-handed

with no excuse, and the Prime will know. He doesn't seem the forgiving type. Niles will pay for this. He could have let me steal the hover, or I could have hit him over the head, or—or *something*. But no, he dumps me with my ticket out and drives off.

The boy isn't stupid; he'll have planned an excuse.

The Prime isn't stupid, either.

I kick the floor, but it's not thick enough or satisfactory and Niles doesn't feel any of it. So I walk to the wing instead. It grows bigger the closer I get, looms sleek impossibility.

Does he think I know how to fly? And I'd have learned that skill where? Because obviously I had one of these in my back pocket growing up. Hell, I've never even been in a private flightwing.

Autopilot, idiot, my brain snaps. *It's not data science.*

The low wings slope forward, barely clear my head as I walk under. I tap the keypass's emblem again, because that's what they do on the feedshows.

It works. A tall panel in the wing's side slides into itself. A compact metal ladder slides out below and uncurls. I half expect some uniformed orderly to jump out and bow with a reverent "my lady."

Somebody will notice this missing, probably the Prime, and the first person he'll look to will be the last one in my company.

Stupid, so stupid. The boy will get himself killed.

I climb the ladder. It retreats in on itself, the door closing without any help from me. I'm in a brushed silver hall, narrow and packed with sliding doors on each side, labeled in digiscreens. Restroom, storage, bunk, icer. I follow the hall right, step through the open arch to the cockpit. Two seats, and a wide console with three data-filled screens and shiny lights.

Double shit.

I take a chair and say, as all the feedshow flyers do, "Engine on."

The wing hums to life, dim lights rising. The data in the central screen disappears, replaced by a pretty woman in a purple flight cap.

"Welcome to the Greypiper 400. I am Pali, the lead connector to your interface." Her nod is almost a bow, dark curls brushing her ears. "Shall I perform a preflight check before we get under way?"

"Uh, sure?"

The screen freezes a beat, Pali caught open-mouthed, then she blinks and smiles. "Preflight check initiated. Estimated completion time, fifteen minutes."

Well, that was easy.

I dig through Niles's pack for the box. It's light, fits in my palm with room to spare, old wood with old hinges. I pop the lid.

Inside beats Yonni's heart.

Snug in a bed of cushioned black. Probably Decker's doing. Beside it lies a cheap audio note tag, small and square with *Listen!* emblazoned on one side. We used them all the time at work, to identify lockers or belongings. I press my thumb to the letters and hold until the note plays.

"I found this with the bracelet." Niles. Clipped, rushed. "I hope it's the right one. The pendant? Your grand-mother's? I didn't realize you meant a *heart* heart. If you're listening to this, Dad has you now, or had you, so you know about me. And the bracelet. I had to give him something. You were becoming too interesting to him, he needed a—" He hesitates and grinds out the words, "a different toy. I'll have everything ready. Reds, ID, a wing—you have to leave the city. You cannot stay on-planet. Dad will find you, and I can't get you out a second time. No one fools Dad twice. Not even me." Silence. Seconds of it, tinny and static, building under my skin. "Not that I wouldn't try. I would. Be safe, Kit," he says, and the message clicks off.

Safe? *Safe?* As if he wasn't my safety. The only thing that felt real in this whole week of hell.

I bite my lip, but I still feel him. Everywhere. The mem-ory, the lack. The Prime's son who's playing martyr to save my life.

Or else just playing.

I am *not* a toy. The Prime never looked at me like a person.

It's a damn dangerous game. Assuming Niles's dad doesn't suss him out, the Brinkers will. And with me gone and not mapped, the Brinkers will have a field day with my family. Hell, with me gone, the Prime might jump on that, too—map Dad and Dee just for the hell of it.

The countdown on the central console screen reaches ten.

Don't think I don't know what her digivirus is doing, the Prime had said. *Why she chose the Archive.*

The Archive held the central data structure of our House, the core network all other networks fed into. A virus begun in the Archive could leech into every data feed House-wide. Networks, public feed stations, secure databases, personal and corporate information stores. Everything.

Mom's smiling face in the pet shop window, red lips blowing into cupped hands. *The question is a matter of heart.*

I didn't realize you meant a heart *heart,* Niles had said.

I lift Yonni's pendant out of the box. It dangles from my fingers, pulses soft between its vines as I twist it back and forth. It's seamless but for the soft glow of the circuits. No buttons to push or spring to pop.

You're a smart girl, it's not hard.

"Mom?" I ask. "Millie Oen?"

Nothing.

"If you think I'm busting the last of Yonni open for you, you are so wrong."

The glow doesn't rise or the pulse skip. It is as it always was, and suddenly I know.

"But I don't have to, do I?"

steal some. Pali flew me to the closest store, and breaking in wasn't an issue with the power-out.

After, we head into North 8th—which is to East 5th what East 5th is to Low South, only less populated. A day's walk that takes us all of ten minutes. I tell Pali to power down her lights flying in, and she docks us in an empty public lot. At least, the map on the screen says it's a public lot. I can't see shit.

Hopefully, with the flightwing being black, no one will see us.

I enter the hall and seal off the cockpit so no light will leak. Then I sit on the cold floor and lay out the heart, the pocket light, and the freshener sticks. I could sniff my way through the box, but the names are straightforward, so I start there.

Metallic Seafron, Sweet Nightsnip, Burnt Ash.

I flip the switches in the base of their tall cylinders, and wait.

Nightsnip kicks in first. Too sweet, almost sticky. I swap it for Pale Pretty, which promises sweet floral undertones. The Seafron's spot-on, though, and the Ash. Pale Pretty kicks in, and the hall smells like nothing so much as blood.

Yonni's heart lifts, literally lifts out of its little box. Rises until it reaches chest level, where it hovers and glows red.

Then Mom sits crossed-legged before me, heart hanging from her neck. "There you are."

She is concentrated light and scan lines. Almost solid, but breaking into dots as she moves. Her hair is still swept high, but little ribbons have fallen over her ears and face. Her purple blouse is open at the neck, her bright eyes tired and a little red.

This recording must have come after the others. She looks human. Normal.

I trail my fingers through her digital cheek and feel nothing.

"Mom."

She smiles. "I'm assuming you followed the clues. Sorry for the protracted trail. It is surprisingly difficult to leave a secret message for one person alone. I miss the days when we could simply hide things in trees. Hollowed, of course." The corner of her mouth bunches, bitten, a little wistful. "You never had the experience, did you? I never took you to the woods to play. Or anywhere really, did I? Not that you will ever know my woods. Those are long, long since gone."

The words trail, tired. She looks tired and old.

I cross my arms. "What do you want?"

The scan lines of her face bounce, blink, her body freezing a beat too long before the humanity kicks in. She doesn't move or answer but is still somehow present—eyes distant, lips pressed, not glitched but silent.

"The question is, what do *you* want?" she says at last. "I don't know, so you'll have to tell me. You can do that through precision."

"That makes no sense," I say.

The scan lines fuzz again, and this time Mom shifts position between one blink and the next—back straighter, hands in her lap. "I made this program on the fly, in between my central project, so there will be glitches. Also, I haven't the time for a full-voice map structure with a broad response range. I will try to answer the most pressing questions, and have recorded some nonrelevant material, but I am not a computer or digital intelligence who can respond to all words and phrasing. This is me, Kit. Just me. You have to be precise." Her smile slips through the exhaustion. "You're smart enough."

Games and more games.

"Really?" I cross my arms, nails digging sharp. "How you figure?"

Fuzzed lines, blinked light, Mom. "I made this program on the fly, in between—"

"No, stop," I say.

She does, frozen between frames.

We face each other, both crossed-legged, knees almost touching. Yonni would sit on the floor with me, just like this.

She'd do my makeup or braid my hair or tell me secrets.

Mom and I never swapped secrets. We aren't now. Info from a light-scanned cutout doesn't count.

"Precise." I rub my temples, fingers stiff, head aching. "Right. And what precisely was your goal with this?"

"Simple," says Mom. "Retribution. Annihilate the House of Galton as we have been annihilated. Gut them from the inside out. And what better way than through their centralized digital core."

The assurance, the smugness, the self-righteous undercurrent of every clipped syllable—

There's lead in my stomach and gauze in my throat. "The power's gone for good, isn't it? Not just here, but House-wide. That's what the virus was about. You've somehow managed to burn the whole system."

Mom smiles, a truly beautiful thing. "That's my girl. Though, there's more than one virus, and more to it than power—of the electronic kind. Remember, be precise."

I almost throw Niles's satchel at her. "Quit with the games, already! This isn't funny. Do you care at all what's at stake? *Who's* at stake?"

Fuzz, blink. I brace for the lecture in map structures and response ranges.

"The question is, what do *you* want? I don't know, so you'll have to tell me. You can do that through precision."

She'll tell me what I want to know, only if I know to ask.

"I hate you," I say.

"I know." Quiet, absolute, and real. Entirely too real. She could be flesh and bone, with her offer of secrets.

I am not going to cry. I'm going to think.

"So there's a second virus?" I ask.

"Yes."

No elaboration. Of course not.

"And it's not about power?"

Fuzz, blink. "I made this program—"

"Stop!"

She does.

I'm going to kill her.

She's already dead.

My chest twists too many stupid ways, and I press my fists to the floor.

Precision, Kit.

"And the second virus isn't about power?" I clip the words, space them out.

"Oh no," says Mom. "It is all about power, but not all power is energy." There it is, the assurance again, the self-righteous traces. She's elegant and sleek and full of the power she describes.

Just like the Prime.

He said he knew why she destroyed the Archive, that

her real project was never about destroying the grid.

And Mom had said something, in one of the dreams. Not destroying, but "rewriting."

The Archive controls information, the repository of the House complete with histories on everyone—us, the lordlings, even bloodlings—our heritage, our line.

Mrs. Divs said something about my line, that I looked like it and Dad sullied it.

Mrs. Divs was an Accountant, like Mom.

"Who are you?" I ask, but that isn't right. "Who were you, before your planet fell? Who were you on Casendellyn?"

Mom fazes out, dotted lines remerging into a new position. She sits on her heels, back straight, hands in her lap. "I am Millisant Evantell Runellen, granddaughter of the High Lord Amanant Fenshia Runellen, ruler of Casendellyn—oldest of the Independents. Our line predates the Galton and Westlet, rivaled only by the House of Fane. You are Kreslyn Amanant Runellen, Heir to the Casendellyn court." She hesitates, smile slipping in and out. "I haven't said that aloud since the gutting. Oen was my mother's middle name."

Oh . . . shit.

Have you ever seen the future, Kit? Mom had said in that dream. *Have you ever had a moment where, without any evidence whatsoever, you just knew?*

And I do.

"You're turning me into a bloodling," I say. "You destroyed the Archive to get rid of any physical DNA back-ups, because it's the only place in the House where they keep it, and you're using the second virus to rewrite the digital bloodling files. You're turning me into the next Heir."

Mom closes her eyes and exhales a sigh so deep her body nearly collapses with it. "That's my girl."

It's perfect, simple. Galton gutted her planet, but Casendellyn was only *one* planet. Galton has one hundred and nine. How then to return the favor?

Why, annihilate their data structure and hijack the Lordship.

Mom, years ago, at the kitchen table. *The Accounting. I've cracked it.*

Her digital image blurs out and a space scene takes her place. A three-dimensional planet, twined in clouds and black slender flight stations. The same fuel extraction vid the Brinkers showed me.

"This is, was, home," Mom voices over, as the stations start to spin. "Galton invaded when I was seven. Most of our population was on-planet when the extraction began. For thirty years, Galton has powered its cities with our blood. No longer. They will be held to Account."

My chest is a void, the narrow hall a hell of ghosts and history. I can't watch, can't look.

"Was I—" I stop. Precision. "Was making me a bloodling always part of the plan?"

"No." Mom reappears and leans forward, elbows on knees. "That idea came with Lord Galton's death." She hesitates. "No, it came to me the moment you marched into my office, demanding treatment for Ricky's mother. You looked so much like my grandfather—the determination, the *power*. The willingness to accept any consequence. You were meant to rule, Kit. You understand cost."

"No," I say, or maybe mouth since she doesn't stop.

"But it wasn't until after Yonni's death, when you kept your bargain and didn't blow my cover or make more demands, that I knew you could be trusted. And it wasn't until the Lord's death that I saw the way to make it happen—bring the story full circle. I've never believed in fate, but this?" She reaches out, hand brushing my cheek as if she knows where I am. "This has me converted. You were always meant to rule, Kit." Her fingers drop to the heart at her neck. "I left an override script in the blackout virus. You can stop it now or let it run as you so choose. Rebuild your House from a dark wasteland, or reclaim the grids before the virus completes and there's no getting them back. Not ideal, I know, but you're a bloodling now. When you say rise, the House stands as one."

"No." I jump up and away from her, back slamming into

the cockpit door. "You can't—no. Stop. End transmission." I kick the air-freshener sticks over, grab Yonni's heart from her neck. "I won't be your devastation, I won't be you."

She pops out like a bubble, taking the light with her.

I'm alone in the dark.

I REINSTATE THE LIGHTS AND PACE THE FLIGHTWING'S tiny hall. Up, down, up, down, my head shaking until my brain rattles like a ball.

The data structure blown, grids House-wide forever busted, me the Heir to make up for it—how is this a legacy? How is this something I'd want?

I stop and slam my fist into the wall. It hurts, so I do it again.

Everyone, *everyone*, has a plan.

Mom will "give me the world" on a blood-strewn plate. The Prime will map me, Niles will stop him at the expense of himself, and the Brinkers will kill off everyone with my blood—my lesser-than-thou nonroyal blood—that they can get their hands on just to prove a point. Like Mom's trying to prove a point, and Niles, and hell, even the Prime.

Do this or die. Do this or *they'll* die.

Do this, or I'll get myself killed for you.

You were always meant to rule, Kit.

"Really? Then maybe you should have stuck around for the last ten years teaching me how!"

I kick the wall. It doesn't care.

I have more bruises than the wing at this point. Serves me right. None of this is the flightwing's fault.

I drop to the floor and stare at Yonni's heart. It beats in its box, quiet and innocent. No one would suspect. No one would even dream.

Think, Kit.

The Prime thought he could reinstate power soon, that it wouldn't be difficult. He doesn't know Mom. With or without power, he'll probably try to take over the House.

What had Niles said? *Even if your mom blew ten Archives, she couldn't touch my dad.*

Lady Galton okayed the gutting of the Brinkers' home planet, so as far as integrity goes, she's on level with the Prime. The bloodling Heir is lost to the abyss, since the records point to me.

There has to be another out.

I breathe deep, switch on the fresheners, and wait for Mom to show.

She does. Soft mouth, soft eyes. "There you are."

"Tell me about the virus override," I say. "And how you're controlling the feeds."

MOM SAID I HAVE TO BE IN RANGE OF THE CENTRAL grid. So I stand on the southern end of the Gilken Tower, bare toes curled over the roof edge, hair bound tight so it doesn't blow. It's breezy up here. Dark below, dark above. The cloudsuites with backup generators thrive in glow-dotted harmony, while the rest of the city looks on in shadow. Traffic whirs, private flightwings, and panic. Not here, though. This street is as dead as the tower under my feet.

The flightwing fills the rooftop at my back. I don't know how the hell Pali landed it in the space, but she managed. Definitely worth her weight in hardware. It's probably not the safest or most secure vantage, but I know this roof—where it is in proximity to the blown Archive and the city's power grid.

More than that, I know the view.

I switch on the three freshener sticks sticking out of my side pants pocket. Metallic Seafin. Burnt Ash.

Energized Renewal.

I had to be very precise indeed to get the name of the last one.

I rub Yonni's heart. It beats with the blood in my ears as the scents trigger the implanted receptor, then transmit the override signal to the grid. It burns, hot and hotter, glows bright between my fingers.

I balance on the pads of my feet and focus on the sky-tower cluster near Low South's Market, with the giant ad-screens that can probably be seen from space.

"Transmit override code K581M," I say. "Project me as Millie Oen and restart the grid."

The city blazes. A thousand windows and streetlights rocketing to life.

I let go of the heart. "Begin projection."

Mom's face appears everywhere—in shop windows and digitized street signs, on the massive ad-screens half a district away.

I tip my head and so does she, in tandem.

Right, let's do this.

"Do I have your attention?" I say and she echoes in an all-encompassing boom. "Excellent."

She smiles and so do I.

"I was hired by the Prime to eradicate the true bloodling line. I was supposed to destroy all physical DNA records, which meant destroying the Archive. This, I did. Those deaths are on my head."

I won't pass that responsibility off, not even on the Prime.

"It was wrong. I should never have taken the job, listened to the Prime. I should have had the courage to stand against him. It may be too little too late, but I'm standing now. The only DNA you'll find in the official bloodling records is mine. So unless you want me as your next Heir and House Lady, I suggest you rework your governmental structure and sort out your shit."

I lean back and fold my arms, which has Mom glaring on-screen. "Also, as soon as this message wraps up, I'm reinstating the blackout everywhere except the Outer Brink. This whole House runs on stolen energy bought with blood. Lord Galton harvested the independents with their populations still *on-planet*, and we all just stood by and watched. And his wife? Lady Galton? She plans to do the same thing to our own people, to the planets on the Brink—which is why they get to keep their energy, and you don't."

Softer, under my breath, I add, "Project indie loop."

Mom's face evaporates under the weight of two dueling images—the destruction of Casendellyn, and the flight stations lining up around the Brinker's planet.

"The left feed is thirty years old; meet the last independent we gutted for fuel. The feed on the right was shot last week; it's the Outer Brink planet Lady Galton wants to gut. You might want to pay attention, it'll play nonstop for everyone running backup generators until someone learns to give a shit."

Everyone without generators won't be powering anything.

I close my eyes. Soak in space and city, energy and heat.

I should stop here. If I had any brain at all, I'd stop here.

"And—" I swallow twice and try again. "And for every-one who maybe isn't a complete asshole—assuming they could go anywhere and be anything—there might be a sticky roll somewhere in Our Divinity. Come eat your weight in sugar."

I fist my hand around Yonni's heart and hold it close to mine.

"Kill the grid," I say and the city blacks out.

HELLO,
WORLD

H E DOESN'T COME.

It's cold in the House of Westlet, or at least in their capital. Their streets are green and, well, *green*. Trees grow everywhere. Along thoroughfares, between towers, sometimes *inside* towers—surrounded by flowers on the other side of multilevel windows, and walkways of fitted stones with swirls etched along the edge in endless detail.

Total waste of someone's time and effort.

But pretty though.

The shopfronts mirror the walkways, clean and ornate. There are four shops this side of Old Town's skytower. Three boutiques and a bakery. I know. I've been by them every day for two weeks.

The old woman with the jewelry shop waves when she sees me. I huddle into my new Westlet hoodie—green, of course—and wave back. Another few steps, and the painted sign of Our Divinity Bakery swings overhead. My feet falter, like always, but I've had some practice now.

Speed is everything.

I grab the door handle and swing it open between one breath and the next. Scan the room before my heart can rise too high.

It skyrockets anyway.

The shop isn't empty.

But everyone is fair. No mop-y black hair swishes over dark eyes and lanky limbs. There are no males, period. Only a high glass bakery case with every sweet thing under the sun, shelves of tea and spices left and right, and two women at the counter.

No one else.

I step inside. Soft painted florals wind over the walls and down to the floor, tracing my steps. Someone must have done them by hand, and here I am walking all over them.

The woman behind the counter, Hannah—who has a daughter about my age and a dog named Mitts—retrieves a sticky roll from the case and a plate from a low shelf.

The girl on this side looks like she's been through hell and not long ago, either, judging by her skinned head and impressive scar—a starburst of multilayered rivets that take up half her skull. She digs through her pockets as Hannah lays the plate on the counter. Each one comes up empty.

Hannah waits, patient, but it's obvious and the silence gets long. Finally, Rivets gives up and stands to attention, like a soldier called to task.

"Forgive me," she says. "It seems I—"

"I've got it," I say.

Rivets spins, which is apparently a bad idea. It almost upends her. She weaves, blinking.

I slide up to the counter and link my arm through hers. "Sorry, I'm late. Hey, Hannah. Any pinenuts today?"

All of Hannah's sticky rolls are worth jumping Houses for, but the pinenuts shame the rest.

Hannah lights up like I've just given her the moon and leans across the counter. "So is this who you've been waiting for?"

My smile freezes. Paste on my skin, glue in my heart. "Absolutely, who else? Can I have that sticky roll?"

Hannah gently pats my hand, because I am 100 percent convincing, then retrieves another plate and roll and pushes them across the counter. "On the house."

"You're going to go belly up if you keep handing me free things," I say.

"Well, that's my choice now, isn't it?" She peers down her nose, which would work better without the accompanying wink.

People are . . . weird in Westlet.

"Thanks." I grab the plates and turn to Rivets. "Inside or out?"

She watches like I'm the weird one. "Out."

We unlink and she moves ahead to open the door. The shopside garden is green, treed, and empty. Three small tables fill the patio, with woven metal legs and chairs. It's too cold to be outside. The breeze too brisk, the air too clean.

I sit here most days.

Rivets has some trouble with her chair, but not too much. I don't pretend not to notice, but I don't comment.

She smiles. "Am I going to mess with your date?"

I wish people wouldn't ask. I hate it when they ask. I hate that they somehow even know to ask.

"He's not going to show," I say. "So no, you won't."

If he was coming, he'd have shown by now.

Niles doesn't play games. Not those kind. Not the ones that jack with a person's soul just because.

I shake my head.

Like I would know. He lied the entire time we were together—which, how long was that exactly?

Yonni would have a fit.

She'd be right.

I rip into my sticky roll.

"You should dump him," says Rivets.

"I'd have to get the chance first."

"Want me to track him down?" She lays a forearm on the table and leans in, wags blonde eyebrows. "I've got con-nections."

"I'd rather kill him myself."

"Just saying, if you ever need a fighter convoy, I'll bring a House-worth of wings to bear."

My eyebrows rise. "Well, *I* have a magical amulet that can power down a whole House on a whim, so I think I'm covered."

"In that case, you should join my unit. I could use a good amulet bearer." Her grin upends her face, light and happy and very young. Infectious and almost catching.

But I remain deadpan, bowing over my plate. "Say the word, and I will clutch my heart and call down curses from afar."

"So it was the heart. I wondered," says a soft voice at my elbow. My head snaps round.

Niles.

Dressed for the weather in a long gray jacket that hits his thighs and a pale white scarf. Hair flustered, hands in pockets, dark eyes as upended as Rivets's smile.

"Makes for a pretty potent amulet," he says.

"Niles," I say. It hangs, suspended.

I'm suspended. The world breathless in an eye of calm.

"Kit." The perfect balance of *K* and *T*.

Somewhere, hurricanes wail.

"Seems like I need another coffee." Rivets's chair scrapes back and she stands, careful. Takes her plate. "Yell if you need a convoy."

"All right," I half whisper. Maybe it's just in my head.

Niles holds out his hand as she rounds the table. "I'm Niles, by the way."

Her face warms, letters tripping off her tongue. "W— Suzanna."

A quick shake, then she disappears through the walk-way gate.

It's just Niles.

And me.

"You came," I say.

"I thought that was the idea."

"Took you long enough."

He moves, hand grasping my chair back as he bends to glare from two inches away. "*The sticky roll of our divinity?* Could you be any more obscure? You know how many divinity shops are in this damn city? And what the hell is up with all these trees?"

His breath warms the chill air, the frosted edges of my mouth. I don't know how he sees through all those bangs.

"Is Niles even your name?" I ask.

"Yes," he says. "Now."

"And it's just that easy?"

His teeth catch the edge of his lip. I could totally do that for him.

"No," he says. "The House is a wreck, there's no power except on the Brink, and Dad figured out what I'd done—which could have gone very badly, if the city hadn't gone mad and swarmed our complex to claim his head."

"You all right?" I ask.

"I'm here, aren't I?" he says.

"That's good," I say.

The silences bends, tightens. Neither of us move.

His eyes squeeze close. "Do you want me here, Kit? Did I read that wrong?"

"Depends," I say.

His eyes snap open, intent with possibility, a wave I won't survive.

I don't know that I want to.

"Is this a game" I ask. "Or will it mean something this time?"

"Are you crazy?" He cups my face in his palms. "I just burned every bridge I had for you. It meant something *every* time," he says, and kisses me.

Words can't express the dead space between isolation and having one ally. Four may be twice two, but two is not twice one. Two is two thousand times one.

—*Scholar Gilken*

AUTHOR'S NOTE

In another universe—where Pluto is happily still a planet—Scholar Gilken was born Gilbert Keith Chesterton and lived from 1874 to 1936. He wrote everything from mysteries to poetry to theological works. Gilken's history exists only in Kit's world, but his quotes are founded in Chesterton's. When I was nine, I found the audio version of *The Innocence of Father Brown* and fell down the rabbit hole. If you are interested in learning more of the man and his work, that's where I'd begin.

ACKNOWLEDGMENTS

Mom, who remembers.

Victoria Marini, who never gives up.

Andrea Cascardi, who follows through.

Janet Johnson, who gives wholeheartedly.

Heidi Sennett, who weaves wisdom with hope.